Short Stories of the American Witch and Witchcraft

British Library Cataloguing-in-Publication Data
A catalogue record for this book is available from
the British Library

Contents

Short Biographies of the Authors

THE SPELL OF WITCHCRAFT

P. T. Barnum

＊

Witchcraft is one of the most baseless, absurd, disgusting and silly of all the humbugs. And it is not a dead humbug either; it is alive, busily exercised by knaves and believed by fools all over the world. Witches and wizards operate and prosper among the Hottentots and negroes and barbarous Indians, among the Siberians and Kirgishes and Lapps, of course. Everybody knows *that* – they are poor ignorant creatures! Yes: but are the French, and Germans, and English, and Americans poor ignorant creatures too? They are, if the belief and practice of witchcraft among them is any test; for in all those countries there are witches. I take up one of the New York City dailies of this very morning, and find in it the advertisements of seven witches. In 1858, there were in full blast in New York and Brooklyn sixteen witches and two wizards. One of these wizards was a black man; a very proper style of person to deal with the black art.

Witch, means a woman who practises sorcery under an agreement with the devil, who helps her. Before the Christian era, the Jewish witch was a mere diviner, or at most a raiser of the dead, and the Gentile witch was a poisoner, a maker of philtres or love potions, and a vulgar sort of magician. The devil part of the business did not begin until a good while after Christ. During the last century or so, again, while witchcraft has been extensively believed in, the witch has degenerated into a very vulgar and poverty-stricken sort of conjuring woman. Take our New York City witches, for instance. They live in cheap and dirty streets that smell bad; their houses are in the same style, infected with a strong odour of cabbage, onions, washing-day, old dinners, and other merely sublunary smells. Their rooms are very ill furnished, and often beset with wash-tubs, swill-pails, mops ,and soiled clothes; their personal appearance is commonly unclean, homely, vulgar, coarse and ignorant, and often rummy. Their fee is a quarter or half of a dollar. Sometimes a dollar. Their divination is worked by cutting and dealing cards or studying the palm of your hand. And the things which they tell you are the most silly and shallow babble in the world; a mess of phrases worn out over and over again. Here is a specimen, as gabbled to the customer over a pack of cards laid out on the table; anybody can do the like: 'You face a misfortune. I think it will come upon you within three weeks, but it may not. A dark-complexion man faces your life-card. He is plotting against you, and you must beware of him. Your marriage-card faces two young women, one fair and the other dark. One you will have, and the other you will not. I think you will have the fair one. She favours the dark-complexioned man, which means trouble. You face money, but you must earn it. There is a good deal, but you may not get much of it,'etc., etc. These words are exactly the sort of stuff that is sold by the witches of today.

Other countries are favoured in like manner. I have not just now the most recent information, but in the year 1857 and 1858, for instance, mobbing and prosecutions growing out of a popular belief in witchcraft were quite plentiful in various parts of Europe. No less than eight cases of the kind in England alone were reported during those two years. Among them was the actual murder of a woman as a witch by a mob in Shropshire; and an attack by another mob in Essex, upon a perfectly inoffensive person, on suspicion of having 'bewitched' a scolding, ill-conditioned girl from which attack the mob was diverted with much difficulty, and thinking itself very unjustly treated. Some others of those cases show a singular quantity of credulity among people of respectability.

While, therefore, some of us may perhaps be justly thankful for safety from such horrible follies as these, still we cannot properly feel very proud of the progress of humanity, since, after not less than six thousand years of existence, and eighteen hundred of revelation, so many believers in witchcraft still exist among the most civilised nations.

It is worth while to print in plain English for my readers a good selection of the very words which have been believed, or are still believed, to possess magic power. Then, any who choose, may operate by themselves, or may put some bold friend up in a corner, and blaze away at him or her until they are wholly satisfied about the power of magic.

The Roman Cato, so famous for his grimness and virtue, believed that if he were ill, it would much help him, and that it would cure sprains in others, to say over these words: 'Daries, dardaries, astaris, ista, pista, sista'; or, as another account has it, 'motas, daries, dardaries, astaries'; or, as still another account says, 'Huat, huat, huat; ista, pista, sista; domiabo, damnaustra.' And sure enough, nothing is truer, as any physician will tell you, that if the old censor only believed hard enough, it would almost certainly help him; not by the force of the words, but by the force of his own ancient Roman imagination. Here are some Greek words of no less virtue: '*Aski, Kataski, Tetrax.*' When the Greek priests let out of their doors those who had been completely initiated in the Eleusinian mysteries, they said to them last of all the awful and powerful words, '*Konx, ompax.*' If you want to know what the usual result was, just say them to somebody, and you will see instantly. The ancient Hebrews believed that there was a secret name of God, usually thought to be inexpressible, and only to be represented by a mystic figure kept in the Temple, and that if anyone could learn it, and repeat it, he could rule the intelligent and unintelligent creation at his will. It is supposed by some that Jehovah is the word which stands for this secret name; and some Hebraists think that the word 'Yahveh' is much more nearly the right one. The Mohammedans, who have received many notions from the Jews, believe the same story about the secret name of God, and they think it was engraved on Solomon's signet, as all readers of the *Arabian Nights* will very well remember. The Jews believed that if you pronounced the word 'Satan', any evil spirit that happened to be by could in consequence instantly pop into you if he wished, and possess you, as the devils in the New Testament possessed people.

Some ancient cities had a secret name, and it was believed that if their enemies could find this out, they could conjure with it so as to destroy such cities. Thus, the secret name of Rome was Valentia, and the word was very carefully kept, with the intention that none should know it except one or two of the chief pontiffs.

Mr Borrow, in one of his books, tells about a charm which a gipsy woman knew and which she used to repeat to herself as a means of obtaining supernatural aid when she happened to want it. This was, 'Saboca enrecar Maria ereria.' He induced her, after much effort, to repeat the words to him, but she always wished she had not, with an evident conviction that some harm would result. He explained to her that they consisted of a very simple phrase, but it made no difference.

An ancient physician, named Serenus Sammonicus, used to be quite sure of curing fevers by means of what he called Abracadabra, which was a sort of inscription to be written on something and worn on the patient's person. It was as follows:

```
A B R A C A D A B R A
  B R A C A D A B R
    R A C A D A B
      A C A D A
        C A D
          A
```

Another gentleman of the same school used to cure sore eyes by hanging round the patient's neck an inscription made up of only two letters, A and Z; but how he mixed them we unfortunately do not know.

By the way, many of the German peasantry in the more ignorant districts still believe that to write Abracadabra on a slip of paper and keep it with you, will protect you from wounds, and that if your house is on fire, to throw this strip into it will put the fire out.

Many charms or incantations call on God, Christ, or some saints, just as the heathen ones call on a spirit. Here is one for epilepsy that seems to appeal to both religions, as if with a queer proviso against any possible mistake about either. Taking the epileptic by the hand, you whisper in his ear, 'I adjure thee by the sun and the moon and the gospel of today, that thou arise and no more fall to the ground; in the name of the Father, Son, and Holy Ghost.'

A charm for the cramp, found in vogue in some rustic regions, is this:

> *'The devil is tying a knot in my leg,*
> *Mark, Luke, and John, unloose it, I beg*
> *Crosses three we make to ease us –*
> *Two for the thieves, and one for Christ Jesus.'*

Here is another, often used in Ireland, which in the same spirit of superstition and ignorant irreverence uses the name of the Saviour for a slight human occasion. It is to cure the toothache, and requires the repeating of the following string of words:

'St Peter, sitting on a marble stone, our Saviour passing by, asked him what was the matter. "Oh, Lord, a toothache!" "Stand up, Peter and follow me; and whoever keeps these words in memory of me shall never be troubled with a toothache. Amen."'

The English astrologer, Lilly, after the death of his wife, formerly a Mrs Wright, found in a scarlet bag which she wore under her arm, a pure gold 'sigil', or round plate, worth about ten dollars in gold, which the former husband of the defunct had used to exorcise a spirit that plagued him. In case any of my readers can afford bullion enough, and would like to drive away any such visitor, let them get such a plate and have engraved round the edge of one side, 'Vicit Leo de tribus Judæ tetragrammaton +.' Inside this engrave a 'holy lamb'. Round the edge of the other side engrave 'Annaphel', and three crosses, thus: + + +; and in the middle, 'Sanctus Petrus Alpha et Omega.'

The witches have always had incantations, which they have used to make a broomstick into a horse, to kill or to sicken animals and persons, etc. Most of these are sufficiently stupid, and not half so wonderful as one I know, which may be found in a certain mysterious volume, called *The Girl's Own Book*, and which, as I can depose, has often power to tickle children. It is this:

'Bandy-legged Borachio Mustachio, Whiskerifusticus, the bald and brave Bombardino of Bagdad, helped Abomilique Bluebeard Bashaw of Babelmandel beat down an abominable bumblebee at Balsora.'

But to the other witches. Their charms were repeated sometimes in their own language and sometimes in gibberish. When the Scottish witches wanted to fly away to their 'Witches' Sabbath', they straddled a broom-handle, a corn-stalk, a straw, or a rush, and cried out, 'Horse and hattock, in the devil's name!' and immediately away they flew, 'forty times as high as the moon,' if they wished. Some English witches in Somerset used instead to say, 'Thout, tout, throughout, and about,' and when they wished to return from their meeting, they said, 'Rentum, tormentum!' If this form of the charm does not manufacture a horse, or even a saw-horse, then I recommend another version of it, thus:

'Horse and pattock, horse and go!
Horse and pellats, ho, ho, ho!'

German witches said (in High Dutch):

> *'Up and away!*
> *Hi! Up aloft, and nowhere stay!'*

Scottish witches had modes of working destruction to the persons or property of those to whom they meant evil, which were strikingly like the negro obeah or mandinga. One of these was, to make a hash of the flesh of an unbaptised child, with that of dogs and sheep, and to put this goodly dish in the house of the victim, reciting the following rhyme:

> *'We put this until this hame*
> *In our Lord the Devil's name;*
> *The first hands that handle thee,*
> *Burned and scalded may they be!*
> *We will destroy houses and hald,*
> *With the sheep and not* (i.e. *cattle*) *into the fauld;*
> *And little shall come to the fore* (i.e. *remain*),
> *Of all the rest of the little store.'*

Another, used to destroy the sons of a certain gentleman named Gordon was, to make images for the boys, of clay and paste, and put them in a fire, saying:

> *'We put this water among this meal*
> *For long pining and ill heal,*
> *We put it into the fire*
> *To burn them up stook and stour* (i.e. *stack and band*)
> *That they be burned with our will,*
> *Like any stikkle* (*stubble*) *in a kiln.'*

In case any lady reader finds herself changed into a hare, let her remember how the witch Isobel Gowdie changed herself from hare back to woman. It was by repeating:

> *'Hare, hare, God send thee cure!*
> *I am in a hare's likeness now;*
> *But I shall be woman even now –*
> *Hare, hare, God send thee care!'*

About the year 1600 there was both hanged and burned at Amsterdam a poor demented Dutch girl, who alleged that she could make the cattle sterile, and bewitch pigs and poultry by saying to them, 'Turius und Shurius Inturius.' I recommend to say this first to an old hen, and if found useful, it might then be tried on a pig.

Not far from the same time a woman was executed as a witch at Bamberg, having, as was often the case, been forced by torture to make a confession. She said that the devil had given her power to send diseases upon those she hated, by saying complimentary things about them, as 'What a strong man!' 'What a beautiful woman!' 'What a sweet child!' It is my own impression that this species of cursing may safely be tried where it does not include a falsehood.

Here are two charms which the German witches used to repeat to raise the devil within the form of a he goat:

'Lalle, Bachea, Magotte, Baphia, Dajam,
Vagoth Heneche Ammi Nagaz, Adomator
Raphael Immanuel Christus Tetragrammaton
Agra Jod Loi. Konig! Konig!'

The two last words to be screamed out quickly. This second one, it must be remembered, is to be read backward except the two last words. It was supposed to be the strongest of all, and was used if the first one failed:

'Anion, Lalle, Sabolos, Sado, Poter, Aziel,
Adonai Sado Vagoth Agra, Jod,
Baphra! Komm! Komm!'

Just in case the devil stayed too long, he could be made to take himself off by addressing to him the following statement, repeated backward:

'Zellianelle Heotti Bonus Vagotha
Plisos sother osech unicus Beelzebub
Dax! Komm! Komm!'

Which would evidently make almost anybody go away.

A German charm to improve one's finances was perhaps no worse then gambling in gold. It ran thus:

'As God be welcomed, gentle moon –
Make thou my money more and soon!'

To get rid of a fever in the German manner, go and tie up a bough of a tree, saying, 'Twig, I bind thee; fever, now leave me!' To give your ague to a willow tree, tie three knots in a branch of it early in the morning, and say, 'Good morning, old one! I give thee the cold; good morning, old one!' and turn and run away as fast as you can without looking back.

Enough of this nonsense. It is pure mummery. Yet it is

worth while to know exactly what the means were which in ancient times were relied on for such purposes, and it is not useless to put this matter on record; for just such formulas are believed in now by many people. Even in this city there are 'witches', who humbug the more foolish part of the community out of their money by means just as foolish as these.

The Unnamable

H. P. LOVECRAFT

WE WERE SITTING on a dilapidated seventeenth-century tomb in the late afternoon of an autumn day at the old burying ground in Arkham, and speculating about the unnamable. Looking toward the giant willow in the cemetery, whose trunk had nearly engulfed an ancient, illegible slab, I had made a fantastic remark about the spectral and unmentionable nourishment which the colossal roots must be sucking from that hoary, charnel earth; when my friend chided me for such nonsense and told me that since no interments had occurred there for over a century, nothing could possibly exist to nourish the tree in other than an ordinary manner. Besides, he added, my constant talk about 'unnamable' and 'unmentionable' things was a very puerile device, quite in keeping with my lowly standing as an author. I was too fond of ending my stories with sights or sounds which paralyzed my heroes' faculties and left them without courage, words, or associations to tell what they had experienced. We know things, he said, only through our five senses or our religious intuitions; wherefore it is quite impossible to refer to any object or spectacle which cannot be clearly depicted by the solid definitions of fact or the correct doctrines of theology – preferably those of the Congregationalists, with whatever modifications tradition and Sir Arthur Conan Doyle may supply.

With this friend, Joel Manton, I had often languidly disputed. He was principal of the East High School, born and bred in Boston and sharing New England's self-satisfied deafness to the delicate overtones of life. It was his view that only our normal, objective experiences possess any esthetic significance, and that it is the province of the artist not so much to rouse strong emotion by action, ecstasy, and astonishment, as to maintain a placid interest and appreciation by accurate, detailed transcripts of everyday affairs. Especially did he object to my preoccupation with the mystical and the unexplained; for although believing in the supernatural much more fully than I, he would not admit that it is sufficiently commonplace for literary treatment. That a mind can find its greatest pleasure in escapes from the daily treadmill, and in original and dramatic re-combinations of images usually thrown by habit and fatigue into the hackneyed patterns of actual existence, was something virtually incredible to his clear, practical, and logical intellect. With him all things and feelings had fixed dimensions, properties, causes, and effects; and although he vaguely knew that the mind sometimes holds visions and sensations of far less geometrical, classifiable, and workable nature, he believed himself justified in drawing an arbitrary line and ruling out of court all that cannot be experienced and understood by the average citizen. Besides, he was almost sure that nothing can be really 'unnamable.' It didn't sound sensible to him.

Though I well realized the futility of imaginative and metaphysical arguments against the complacency of an orthodox sun-dweller, something in the scene of this afternoon colloquy moved me to more than usual contentiousness. The crumbling slate slabs, the patriarchal trees, and the centuried gambrel roofs of the witch-haunted old town that stretched around, all combined to rouse my spirit in defense of my work; and I was soon carrying my thrusts into the enemy's own country. It was not, indeed, difficult to begin a counter-attack, for I knew that Joel Manton actually half clung to many old-wives' superstitions which sophisticated people had long outgrown; beliefs in the appearance of dying persons at distant places, and in the impressions left by old faces on the windows through which they had gazed all their lives. To credit these whisperings of rural grandmothers, I now insisted, argued a faith in the existence of spectral substances on the earth apart from and subsequent to their material counterparts. It argued a capability of believing in phenomena beyond all normal notions; for if a dead man can transmit his visible or tangible image half across the world, or down the stretch of the centuries, how can it be absurd to suppose that deserted houses are full of queer sentient things, or that old graveyards teem with the terrible, unbodied intelligence of generations? And since spirit, in order to cause all the manifestations attributed to it, cannot be limited by any of the laws of matter; why is it extravagant to imagine psychically living dead things in shapes – or absences of shapes – which must for human spectators be utterly and appallingly 'unnamable'? 'Common sense' in reflecting on these subjects, I assured my friend with some warmth, is merely a stupid absence of imagination and mental flexibility.

Twilight had now approached, but neither of us felt any wish to cease speaking. Manton seemed unimpressed by my arguments, and eager to refute them, having that confidence in his own opinions which had doubtless caused his success as a teacher; whilst I was too sure of my ground to fear defeat. The dusk fell, and lights faintly gleamed in some of the distant windows, but we did not move. Our seat on the tomb was very comfortable, and I knew that my prosaic friend would not mind the cavernous rift in the ancient, root-disturbed brickwork close behind us, or the utter blackness of the spot brought by the intervention of a tottering, deserted seventeenth-century house between us and the nearest lighted road. There in the dark, upon that riven tomb by the deserted house, we talked on about the 'unnamable,' and after my friend had finished his scoffing I told him of the awful evidence behind the story at which he had scoffed the most.

My tale had been called *The Attic Window*, and appeared in the January, 1922, issue of *Whispers*. In a good many places, especially the South and the Pacific coast, they took the magazines off the stands at the complaints of silly milksops; but New England didn't get the thrill and merely shrugged its shoulders at my extravagance. The thing, it was averred, was biologically impossible to start with; merely another of those crazy country mutterings which Cotton Mather had been gullible enough to dump into his chaotic *Magnalia Christi Americana*, and so poorly authenticated that even he had not ventured to name the locality where the horror occurred. And as to the way I amplified the bare jotting of the old mystic – that was quite impossible, and characteristic of a flighty and notional scribbler! Mather had indeed told of the thing as being born, but nobody but a cheap sensationalist would think of having it grow up, look into people's windows at night, and be hidden in the attic of a house, in flesh and in spirit, till someone saw it at the window centuries later and couldn't describe what it was that turned his hair gray. All this was flagrant trashiness, and my friend Manton was not slow to insist on that fact. Then I told him what I had found in an old diary kept between 1706 and 1723, unearthed among family papers not a mile from where we were sitting; that, and the certain reality of the scars on my ancestor's chest and back which the diary described. I told him, too, of the fears of others in that region, and how they were whispered down for generations; and how no mythical madness came to the boy who in 1793 entered an abandoned house to examine certain traces suspected to be there.

It had been an eldritch thing – no wonder sensitive students shudder at the Puritan age in Massachusetts. So little is known of what went on beneath the surface – so little, yet such a ghastly festering as it bubbles up putrescently in occasional ghoulish glimpses. The witchcraft terror is a horrible ray of light on what was stewing in men's crushed brains, but even that is a trifle. There was no beauty: no freedom – we can see that from the architectural and household remains, and the poisonous sermons of the cramped divines. And inside that rusted iron straitjacket lurked gibbering hideousness, perversion, and diabolism. Here, truly, was the apotheosis of the unnamable.

Cotton Mather, in that demoniac sixth book which no one should read after dark, minced no words as he flung forth his anathema. Stern as a Jewish prophet, and laconically unamazed as none since his day could be, he told of the beast that had brought forth what was more than beast but less than man – the thing with the blemished eye – and of the screaming drunken wretch that they hanged for having such an eye. This much he baldly told, yet without a hint of what came after. Perhaps he did not know, or perhaps he knew and did not dare to tell. Others knew, but did not dare to tell – there is no public hint of why they whispered about the lock on the door to the attic stairs in the house of a childless, broken, embittered old man who had put up a blank slate slab by an avoided grave, although one may trace enough evasive legends to curdle the thinnest blood.

It is all in that ancestral diary I found; all the hushed innuendoes and furtive tales of things with a blemished eye seen at windows in the night or in deserted meadows near the woods. Something had caught my ancestor on a dark valley road, leaving him with marks of horns on his chest and of apelike claws on his back; and when they looked for prints in the trampled dust they found the mixed marks of split hooves and vaguely anthropoid paws. Once a post-rider said he saw an old man chasing and calling to a frightful loping, nameless thing on Meadow Hill in the thinly moonlit hours before dawn, and many believed him. Certainly, there was strange talk one night in 1710 when the childless, broken old man was buried in the crypt behind his own house in sight of the blank slate slab. They never unlocked that attic door, but left the whole house as it was, dreaded and deserted. When noises came from it, they whispered and shivered; and hoped that the lock on that attic door was strong. Then they stopped hoping when the horror occurred at the parsonage, leaving not a soul alive or in one piece. With the years the legends take on a spectral character – I suppose the thing, if it was a living thing, must have died. The memory had lingered hideously – all the more hideous because it was so secret.

During this narration my friend Manton had become very silent, and I saw that my words had impressed him. He did not laugh as I paused, but asked quite seriously about the boy who went mad in 1793, and who had presumably been the hero of my fiction. I told him why the boy had gone to that shunned, deserted house, and remarked that he ought to be interested, since he believed that windows retained latent images of those who had sat at them. The boy had gone to look at the windows of that horrible attic, because of tales of things seen behind them, and had come back screaming maniacally.

Manton remained thoughtful as I said this, but gradually reverted to his analytical mood. He granted for the sake of argument that some unnatural monster had really existed, but reminded me that even the most morbid perversion of nature need not be *unnamable* or scientifically indescribable. I admired his clearness and persistence, and added some further revelations I had collected among the old people. Those later spectral legends, I made plain, related to monstrous apparitions more frightful than anything organic could be; apparitions of gigantic bestial forms sometimes visible and sometimes only tangible, which floated about on moonless nights and haunted the old house, the crypt behind it, and the grave where a sapling had sprouted beside an illegible slab. Whether or not such apparitions had ever gored or smothered people to death, as told in uncorroborated traditions, they had produced a strong and consistent impression; and were yet darkly feared by very aged natives, though largely forgotten by the last two generations – perhaps dying for lack of being thought about. Moreover, so far as esthetic theory was involved, if the psychic emanations of human creatures be grotesque distortions, what coherent representation could express or portray so gibbous and infamous a nebulosity as the specter of a malign, chaotic perversion, itself a morbid blasphemy against nature? Molded by the dead brain of a hybrid nightmare, would not such a vaporous terror constitute in all loathsome truth the exquisitely, the shriekingly *unnamable*?

The hour must now have grown very late. A singularly noiseless bat brushed by me, and I believe it touched Manton also, for although I could not see him I felt him raise his arm. Presently he spoke.

'But is that house with the attic window still standing and deserted?'

'Yes,' I answered. 'I have seen it.'

'And did you find anything there – in the attic or anywhere else?'

'There were some bones up under the eaves. They may have been what that boy saw – if he was sensitive he wouldn't have needed anything in the window-glass to unhinge him. If they all came from the same object it must have been an hysterical, delirious monstrosity. It would have been blasphemous to leave such bones in the world, so I went back with a sack and took them to the tomb behind the house. There was an opening where I could dump them in. Don't think I was a fool – you ought to have seen that skull. It had four-inch horns, but a face and jaw something like yours and mine.'

At last I could feel a real shiver run through Manton, who had moved very near. But his curiosity was undeterred.

'And what about the window-panes?'

'They were all gone. One window had lost its entire frame, and in all the others there was not a trace of glass in the little diamond apertures. They were that kind – the old lattice windows that went out of use before 1700. I don't believe they've had any glass for a hundred years or more – maybe the boy broke 'em if he got that far; the legend doesn't say.'

Manton was reflecting again.

'I'd like to see that house, Carter. Where is it? Glass or no glass, I must explore it a little. And the tomb where you put those bones, and the other grave without an inscription – the whole thing must be a bit terrible.'

'You did see it – until it got dark.'

My friend was more wrought upon than I had suspected, for at this touch of harmless theatricalism he started neurotically away from me and actually cried out with a sort of gulping gasp which released a strain of previous repression. It was an odd cry, and all the more terrible because it was answered. For as it was still echoing, I heard a creaking sound through the pitchy blackness, and knew that a lattice window was opening in that accursed old house beside us. And because all the other frames were long since fallen, I knew that it was the grisly glassless frame of that demoniac attic window.

Then came a noxious rush of noisome, frigid air from that same dreaded direction, followed by a piercing shriek just beside me on that shocking rifted tomb of man and monster. In another instant I was knocked from my gruesome bench by the devilish threshing of some unseen entity of titanic size but undetermined nature; knocked sprawling on the root-clutched mold of that abhorrent graveyard, while from the tomb came such a stifled uproar of gasping and whirring that my fancy peopled the rayless gloom with Miltonic legions of the misshapen damned. There was a vortex of withering, ice-cold wind, and then the rattle of loose bricks and plaster; but I had mercifully fainted before I could learn what it meant.

Manton, though smaller than I, is more resilient; for we opened our eyes at almost the same instant, despite his greater injuries. Our couches were side by side, and we knew in a few seconds that we were in St. Mary's Hospital. Attendants were grouped about in tense curiosity, eager to aid our memory by telling us how we came there, and we soon heard of the farmer who had found us at noon in a lonely field beyond Meadow Hill, a mile from the old burying ground, on a spot where an ancient slaughterhouse is reputed to have stood. Manton had two malignant wounds in the chest, and some less severe cuts or gougings in the back. I was not so seriously hurt, but was covered with welts and contusions of the most bewildering character, including the print of a split hoof. It was plain that Manton knew more than I, but he told nothing to the puzzled and interested physicians till he had learned what our injuries were. Then he said we were the victims of a vicious bull – though the animal was a difficult thing to place and account for.

After the doctors and nurses had left, I whispered an awe struck question:

'Good God, Manton, but *what was it*? Those scars – *was it like that*?'

And I was too dazed to exult when he whispered back a thing I had half expected—

'No – it wasn't that way at all. It was everywhere – a gelatin – a slime – yet it had shapes, a thousand shapes of horror beyond all memory. There were eyes – and a blemish. It was the pit – the maelstrom – the ultimate abomination. Carter, it was the *unnamable!*'

Double Hex

SAMUEL M. CLAWSON

High summer in the Pennsylvania foothills often brings an oppressive humidity even in the coolest hours. It was already stuffy in the little bedroom under the eaves where Amanda Spiegell crouched in the light of a guttered candle, waiting for the dawn to make the cock crow. He was in a slatted box on the roof of the kitchen shed where he could see the low rise of Gobbler's hill to the east of Hummerstown.

She listened intently for any sound of her brother, Reuben, stirring in the second-floor bedroom directly beneath. If he guessed the cock was there, he'd surely know that she meant to strike at dawn when the tide of life is at full ebb, and he'd lay the cock still with his hex spell. The message in the tea leaves had been clear enough. A death in the family before the dark of the moon was done. There were only her and Reuben locked in the dark battle of hex and spell. The stark pattern in the bottom of the divining cup had warned her that the climax was at hand.

A faint greyness relieved the dead black at the window pane at the foot of her bed. The window was raised several inches at the bottom and the soft shuffle of spreading wings against the sides of the cage came to her ears. She crouched lower, bending over the floor. Her forefingers darted downward and inscribed an intricate sign as the cock began the first discordant notes of his call.

'Oh, brother, devil brother,' she spat out the words. 'Fade, pale, choke, smother, Fall, crawl, lie, die.'

A muffled snort from the bedroom below interrupted the last notes of the cock's crow. Amanda remained bent over, listening. She gasped with delight when a thumping crash shook the old structure of the house. Then, as she half rose from her cramped position, knife-like pain stabbed into her back.

The sound she made was an animal compound of surprise and

18

fury. She knew that somehow he had made a doll with a part of her in it. Not finger or toe clippings—she was careful about that. Perhaps a hair or two had escaped from the tight fitting house cap she always wore. There was nothing to be done now. Admitting receipt of a hex-blow only strengthened it tenfold. The knife-like pain had only been a cramp from bending over so long. She formed the thought as her defence, wishing grimly that she could believe it. Go down and fix his breakfast. Of course he carried the doll with him. No use looking for it. She had to crush him before he could use it again.

She pulled the stiff black skirt down over her ample hips, hurried into the blouse and tugged the comb through her iron-grey hair. Reuben's bedroom door was open when she came down the steps from the third floor and passed along the hallway. He had turned from the mirror and was watching when she stopped in the door. She remembered when she saw the costume. It was Wednesday morning. Every Wednesday morning he tried on the long scarlet cape and ugly white headthing with the black flap and eyeholes hanging over his face. She could see his piggy eyes shining behind the black cloth.

'Four eggs, Amanda,' he said thickly through the muffling cloth. 'And get rid of that damn rooster out there, wherever he came from—made me fall over the chair.' She could hear his voice in a diminishing mutter as she went on towards the steps. She felt the old creepy feeling on the nape of her neck and supposed that he was throwing his fateful hex-chant after her. 'Aiya, aiya, simple sister. Boil, burn, break, blister.' When he was alive father had never allowed it but Reuben had always found a time and place to whisper it in her ear.

It seemed years instead of six months since they'd put father in the ground. Reuben was the man and a woman has no say. He'd sold the farm and come to town. Rented a house and taken a job in Krause's butcher shop. Built the hex fire around her by day and by night—by chant and by spell. Oh, she knew the reason why. The money from the farm and what father had left in the bank. Reuben loved money. Every bite she ate was a piece of it—she'd seen it in his eyes.

The house was a spook's hold. He claimed to like it because the blind-alley street out in front ducked between Carter's warehouse and the City Garage to let out in the Main Square. He could whip around the corner and be at his job in Krause's Market in five minutes. Or to the Lodge on the other side of the square for an evening. After supper tonight he'd go up to his room, wrap the costume in a piece of butcher paper and go out to the lodge meeting.

She hated the house. Haunt-heavy and hex-walled. She thought of her Reuben doll, buried in the yard when it had failed her. The cat she had brought to set inside the seventh circle while she cast the death spell. He'd put the devil's horns on it with his thumb and two outside fingers. An hour later the cat had wandered out into the street in front of the house and Smeckler's grocery truck had ground the life out of him.

'Good eggs, Amanda,' Reuben looked up from his plate. 'Why don't you pull up a chair and have some?'

'You know I don't do that,' she said in a flat voice, turning from the stove and her puttering with the skillet. 'The men eat and then the women. Old custom is good enough for me.' She sniffed and went back to scraping at the bottom of the skillet. Why did he always think her a fool? He could put a sign on the egg in the shell or the flour in the bin and no matter. The fire would burn it out at cooking. He would get no chance to see her food between the cooking and the eating. Especially not now with the foot of the reaper already on the door sill.

'The trouble with you, Amanda, you're dumb as an ox.' Reuben sucked audibly at the cup of coffee and glanced at her back with a frown on his butcher's face. 'Hex is not for the likes of you so stop fooling with it. Some day you'll put the sign on yourself if you don't take care.'

'There's no money in the food jar,' she said coldly without looking around. 'Will you drop something in or bring some of Krause's horse flesh if you want to eat that.'

'We sell good meat.' He scowled at the thought of parting with money. 'Besides, I meant to tell you. We close the market for tomorrow. Krause and me are going rabbit hunting while they put the new counters in. Then you can make us a great big hassenpfeffer.'

After Reuben had gone she fried eggs and potatoes and sat at the table chewing nervously. Her eyes kept wandering to the wholesale meat company calendar on the far wall. She seldom noticed dates but yesterday she had traced the phases of the moon printed beside each day. In three more days—. She heard the front door open and turned to see Reuben standing by the clothes rack in the hallway.

'Damned rooster,' he said gruffly. 'Wondering how he got put up there on the roof and forgot my hat.'

She sat stiffly in the chair until the front door slammed then lifted a forkful of egg toward her mouth. Suddenly she drew in a harsh gasping breath. He'd seen the food. Of course the hex was on it. It must be that he too knew the time was near. Wily as a fox—he had almost trapped her. She snatched up the plate, car-. ried it to the garbage pail and scraped it off hastily.

When Amanda straightened up with the fork and plate still in her hand, her eyes were level with the calendar hanging slightly askew on the wall. Odd, she hadn't known this Wednesday was a red-letter holiday. Realization drenched her with the icy shock of startled fear. It was last month's sheet she was seeing. Her hand rose slowly and lifted the old sheet. The plate slipped from her other hand and shattered on the floor. No wonder he had come back. The new moon was due tonight. This was the day of the reaper forecast in the divining cup.

After the dishes were done she went upstairs to make the beds, her mind hunting wildly for a plan. When she pushed Reuben's door open her eyes went first to the table at the foot of the rumpled bed. It was a plain table with a lamp, an ashtray, and a rack of pipes. She had crocheted the large doily in the middle of the table. The hex sign was worked into it so cleverly that you could only see it by holding the doily up to the light. Sometimes he brushed the doily aside or left it carelessly tossed in the easy chair beside the table where he liked to sit and read. She always put it back to the sign of the devil's horns pointed up across the bed.

This morning the .22 rifle which usually hung on the wall above the bed was lying across the doily. The rifle was freshly oiled. The cleaning rod was leaning against the table and a box of cartridges spilled open beside the rifle. She looked along the barrel and saw that it pointed at Reuben's picture on the bureau. She came up to the table and reached out to lift the rifle. Then she saw that the doily was turned. She knew where the horns of the hex were by the little stitches she had dropped at the edge by each horn tip. The horns lay on each side of the rifle barrel and bracketed the picture on the bureau.

She drew her hand back without touching the rifle. It was a double sign. Strong hex and hard. She made the bed and hurried out of the room. For a while she sat in the kitchen, thinking, weighing, feeling more confident as she reviewed the lay of the hex. After a while she went back into his room and this time noticed that the rifle was loaded and the safety off. For a moment she frowned because this wasn't like Reuben. He was a careful one with a gun. Then she smiled. That was the way with hex. It changed little things—enough.

His dinner was hot in the pans when Reuben came in at five.

Instead of going to the stove and lifting the lids, he just stood there for a minute with his face the colour of a slab of suet. Then he went up the stairs. She heard him tramping around the bedroom like a caged animal. The he called down the stairs for her to come up.

'Get me a glass of schnapps,' he said gruffly when she came to the doorway. He was standing in front of the bureau and she could see his hands shaking all the way across the room.

'Just had a hell of an experience. Went over to Krause's house to look at his new gun. Picked the damn thing up and it went off Clipped through my hair. That close.'

Her mind raced while she went down the stairs and poured a glass on the pantry shelf. Oh yes, devil brother. One horn has missed you but the other is loaded too. Right there on the table. She listened unconsciously for the shattering report in the room above.

'Set it down. I'll get it in a minute,' he said when she came in with the glass. 'First, unload that damn gun, will you? I just noticed, it's loaded too.'

It was like a drench of cold water full in her face. How could both horns of a perfect hex have failed? She picked up the rifle and felt the weight of it in her hands. Almost as though by plan, her finger slipped inside the trigger guard and her hand clenched hard—like she had locked fingers uselessly around the neck of the Reuben doll. This time it was different. The rifle barked and ripped back in her hands. Reuben staggered one step and fell back on the bed.

She swayed forward with the rifle still clutched in her hands. In the ruin of his face where the bullet had found him, Amanda saw victory. She knew his spirit had lifted from him and her thought went flashing to the long knife-like splinter of yew-wood hidden in the bottom of her trunk. She'd saved a gallon of rooster blood to get it from old Granny Merk. Now, drive it through his heart and seal him out of the mortal world forever. She shook her head. It wouldn't do in this case with people coming and all. Anyway, he was the dumb ox—not her. Like mortal, like spirit— he'd never find his way back. She laid the rifle on the table and went down the stairs. A few minutes later she called the police.

It was an hour later and she was rocking back and forth in the old parlour rocker. The front door was open and the place was full of them. Dean, the plain clothes Chief, the coroner, two patrol car men in uniform, and a *Herald* reporter. As usual, Dean was talking.

'Damnedest thing I ever heard of. Picked up one gun over at Krause's place and shot a furrow through his hair. Then he comes home, picks up another, and bingo. You shouldn't have picked up the gun though, Miss Spiegell,' he frowned at Amanda. 'Besides disturbing the evidence, you mighta shot yourself. The rest of the clip was still in there.'

She looked up from her hands twisted together in the folds of the apron she was wearing and saw the flash of colour in the doorway. The squat figure wrapped in the long scarlet cape, the white hooded head, and the black face mask with the little piggy eyes shining behind it.

'Reuben,' her voice shrilled in the earache range. 'Oh damn you. I should have used the splinter.' She slid down into a moaning blubber.

One of the patrol men jerked his pistol from its holster and the masked man hastily pushed his hood back and showed his face. Everyone recognized Bill Stern, the shoe shop proprietor.

'What's going on here?' Stern asked plaintively. 'I just dropped over to ask about Reuben. Saw him sitting in his chair at the meeting. He was pale as a ghost and when I looked again, he'd

Dr. Muncing, Exorcist

GORDON MACCREAGH

The brass plate on the gate post of the trim white wicket said only: Dr. Muncing, Exorcist.

Aside from that, the house was just the same as all the others in that street—semi-detached, whitewashed, respectable. A few more brass plates announced other sober citizens with their sprinkling of doctors of medicine and one of divinity. But Dr. Muncing, Exorcist; that was suggestive of something quite different and strange.

The man who gazed reflectively out of the window at the driving rain, was, like his brass sign, vaguely suggestive, too, of something strange; of having the capacity to do something that the other sober citizens, doctors and lawyers, did not do.

He was of a little more than middle height, broad, with strong, capable-looking hands; his face was square cut, finely criss-crossed with weatherbeaten lines, tanned from much travel in far-away lands; a strong nose hung over a thin, wide mouth that closed with an extraordinary determination.

The face of a normal man of strong character. It was the eyes that conveyed that vague impression of something unusual. Deep set, they were, of an indeterminate colour, hidden beneath a frown of reflective brows; brooding eyes, suggestive of a knowledge of things that other sober citizens did not know.

The other man who stared out of the other window was younger, bigger in every way; an immense young fellow who carried in his big shoulders and clean complexion every mark of having devoted more of his college years to study of football rather than of medicine. This one grunted an ejaculation.

'I'll bet a dollar this is a patient for you.'

Dr. Muncing came over to the other window. 'I don't bet dollars with Dr. James Terry. Gambling seems to have been one

24

of the few things you did really well at Johns College. The fellow does look plentifully frightened, at that.'

The man in question was hurrying down the street, looking anxiously at the house numbers; bent over, huddled in a raincoat, he read the numbers furtively, as though reluctant to turn his head out of the protection of his up-turned collar. He uttered a glad cry as he saw the plate of Dr. Muncing, Exorcist, and, letting the gate slam, he stumbled up the path to the door.

Dr Muncing met the man personally, led him to a comfortable chair, mixed a stimulant for him, offered him a cigarette. Calm, methodical, matter-of-fact, this was his 'bedside manner' with such cases. Forcefully he compelled the impression that, whatever might be the trouble, it was nothing that could not be cured. He stood waiting for an explanation. The man stammered an incoherent jumble of nothings.

'I—Doctor, I don't know how—I can't tell you what it is, but the Reverend Mr. Hendryx sent me to you. Yet I don't know what to tell you; there's nothing to describe.'

'Well,' said the doctor judicially, 'that is already interesting. If there's nothing and if the Reverend Mr. Hendryx feels that he can't pray it away, we probably have something that we can get hold of.'

His manner was dominant and cheerful, he radiated confidence. His bulky young assistant had been chosen for just that purpose also, to assist in putting over the impression of power, of force to deal with queer and horrible things that could not be sanely described.

The man began to respond to that atmosphere. He got a grip on himself and began to speak more coherently.

'Doctor, I don't know what to tell you. There have been no—spooks, or anything of that sort. We've seen nothing; heard nothing. It's only a feeling. I—you'll laugh at me, Doctor, but—it's just a something in the dark that brings a feeling of awful fear; and I know that it will catch me. Last night—my God, last night it almost touched me.'

'I never laugh,' said Dr. Muncing seriously, 'until I have laid my ghost. For some ghosts are horribly real. Tell me something about yourself, your family, your home and so on. And as to your fears, whatever they are, please don't try to conceal them from me.'

A baffled expression came over the man's face. 'There's nothing to tell, Doctor; nothing that's different to anybody else. I don't know what could bring this frightful thing about us. I—my name is Jarrett—I sell real estate up in the Catskills. I have a little place a hundred feet off the paved state road, two miles from the village. There's nothing old or dilapidated about the house; there's modern plumbing, electric lights, and so on. No old graveyards anywhere in the neighbourhood. Not a single thing to bring this horror; and yet—I tell you, Doctor, there's something frightful in the dark that we can feel.'

'Hm-m!' The doctor pursed his lips and walked a short beat, his hands deep in his pockets. 'A new house; no old associations. Begins to sound like an elemental, only how would such a thing have gotten loose? Or it might be a malignant geoplasm, but—Tell me about your family, Mr. Jarrett.'

'There's only four of us, Doctor. There's my wife's brother, who's an invalid; and . . .'

'Ah-h!' A quick breath came from the doctor. 'So there's a sick man, yes? What is his trouble?'

'His lungs are affected. He was advised to come to us for the mountain air; and he was getting very much better; but recently he's very much worse again. We've been thinking that perhaps this constant terror has been too much for him.'

'Hm-m, yes, indeed.' The doctor strode his quick beat back and forth; his indeterminate eyes were distinctly steel grey just now. 'Yes, yes, the terror, and the sick man who grows worse. Quite so. Who else, Mr. Jarrett? What else have you that might attract a visophaging entity?'

'A viso-what? Good God, Doctor, we haven't anything to attract anything. Besides my wife's brother there's only my son, ten years of age, and my wife. She gets it worse than any of us; she says she has even seen—but I think there's a lot of blarney in all that.' The man contrived a sick smile. 'You know how women are, Doctor; she says she has seen shapes—formless things in the dark. She likes to think she is psychic, and she is always seeing things that nobody else knows anything about.'

'Oh, good Lord!' Dr. Muncing groaned and his face was serious. 'Verily do fools rush in. All the requirements for piercing the veil. Heavens, what idiots people can be.'

Suddenly he shot an accusing finger at Mr. Jarrett. 'I suppose she makes you sit round table with her, and all that sort of stuff.'

'Yes, Doctor, she does. Raps and spelt-out messages, and so on.'

'Good Lord!' The doctor walked angrily back and forth. 'Fools by the silly thousand play with this kind of fire, and this time these poor simpletons have broken in on something.'

He whirled on the frightened relator with accusing finger, laying down the law.

'Mr. Jarrett, your foolish wife doesn't know what she has done. I myself don't know what she has turned loose or what this thing might develop into. We may be able to stop it. It may escape and grow into a world menace. I tell you we humans don't begin to know what forces exist on the other side of that thin dividing line that we don't begin to understand. The only thing to do now is to come with you immediately to your home; and we must try and find out what this thing is that has broken through and whether we can stop it.'

The Jarrett house turned out exactly as described. Modern and commonplace in every way; situated in an acre of garden and shrubbery on a sunlit slope of the Catskill Mountains. The other houses of the straggly little village were much the same, quiet residences of normal people who preferred to retire a little beyond the noise and activity of the summer resort of Pine Bend about two miles down the state road.

The Jarrett family fitted exactly into their locale. Well meaning, hospitable rural non-entities. The lady who was psychic was over-plump and short of breath at that elevation; the son, a gangling schoolboy, evinced the shy aloofness of a country youth before strangers; the sick man, thin and drawn, with an irritable cough, showed the unnatural flush of colour on his cheeks that marked his disease.

It required very much less than Dr. Muncing's keenness to see that all of these people were in a condition of nervous tension that in itself was proof of something that had made quite an extraordinary effect on their unimaginative minds.

Dilated eyes, tremulous limbs, backward looks; all these things showed that something had brought this unfortunate family to the verge of a panic that reached the very limits of their control.

The doctor was an adept at dispelling that sort of jumpiness. Such a mental condition was the worst possible for combating 'influences,' whatever they might be. He acknowledged his introductions with easy confidence, and then he held up his hand.

'No, no, nix on that. Give me a chance to breathe. D'you want to ruin my appetite with horrors? Let's eat first and then you can spread yourselves out on the story. No ghost likes a full stomach.'

He was purposely slangy. The immediate effect was that his hosts experienced a measure of relief. The man radiated such an impression of knowledge, of confidence, of power.'

The meal, however, was at best a lugubrious one. Conversation had to be forced to dwell on ordinary subjects. The wife evinced a painful disinclination to go into the kitchen. 'Our cook left us two days ago,' she explained. The boy was silent and frightened.

The sick man said little, and coughed a dry, petulant bark at intervals.

The doctor, engrossed in his plate, chattered gaily about nothing; but all the time he was watching the invalid like a hawk. James Terry did his best to distract attention from the expert's scrutiny of everybody and everything in the room. By the time the meal was over the doctor had formed his opinion about the various characteristics and idiosyncrasies of his hosts, and he dominated the company with his expansive cheerfulness.

'Well, now, let's get one of those satisfying smokes in the jimmy pipe, and you can tell me all about it. You'—selecting the lady—'you tell me. I'm sure you'll give the best account.'

The lady, flustered and frightened, was able to add very little to what her husband had already described. There was nothing to add. A baffling nothingness enshrouded the whole situation; but it was a nothingness that was full of an unnamable fear—a feeling of terror enhanced by the 'shapes' of the wife's psychic imaginings. A nameless nothing to be combated.

The doctor shrugged with impatience. He had met with just such conditions before: the inability of people to describe their ghostly happenings with coherence. He decided on a bold experiment.

'My dear lady,' he said, devoting his attention to the psychic one, 'it is difficult to exorcise a mere feeling until we know something about the cause of it. Now I'll tell you what we ought to do. When you sit at your table for your little seances you get raps and so on, don't you? And you spell out messages from your "spirit friends," isn't it? And you'd like to go into a trance and let your "guides" control you; only you are a little nervous about it; and all that kind of stuff, no?'

'Why, yes, Doctor, that is just about what happens, but how should you know all that?'

'Hm,' grunted the doctor dryly. 'You are not alone in your foolishness, my dear lady; there are many thousands in the United States who take similar chances. They look upon psychic exploration as a parlour game. But now what I want to suggest is, let's have one of your little seances now. And you will go into a trance this time and perhaps you—I mean your guides—will tell us something. In the trance condition, which after all is a form of hypnosis—though we do not know whether the state is auto-induced or whether it is due to the suggestion of an outside influence—in this hypnotic condition the subconscious reflexes are sensitive to influences that the more material conscious mind cannot receive.'

Mrs. Jarrett's plump hand fluttered to her breast. This was so sudden; and she had really been a little bit afraid of her seances since this terror came into the house. But the doctor was already arranging the little round table and the chairs.

Without looking round, he said, 'You need not be at all nervous this time. And I want your brother particularly to stay in the room, though not necessarily at the table. Jimmy, you sit aside and steno whatever comes through, will you.' And in a quiet aside to his friend, he added, 'Sit near the switch, and if I holler, throw on the lights instantly and see that the sick man gets a stimulant. I may be busy.'

Under the doctor's experienced direction everything was soon ready. Just the four sat at the table, the Jarrett family and the doctor. The sick brother sat tucked in an armchair by the window and Jimmy Terry near the light switch at the door.

Once more the doctor cautioned the brawny Terry, "Watch this carefully, Jimmy. I'm putting the sick man's life into your hands. If you feel anything, if you sense anything, if you *think* anything near him, snap on the lights. Don't ask anything. Act. Ready? All right then, black out.'

With the click of the switch the room was in darkness through which came only the petulant cough of the sick man. As the eyes accustomed themselves to the gloom there was sufficient glow from the moonlight outside to distinguish the dim outlines of figures.

'This is what you usually do, isn't it?' asked the doctor. 'Hands on the table and little fingers touching?' And without waiting for the reply of which he seemed to be so sure, he continued, 'All the usual stuff, I see. But now, Mrs. Jarrett, I'm going to lay my hands over yours and you will go into a trance. So. Quiet and easy now. Let yourself go.'

In a surprisingly short space of time the table shivered with that peculiar inward tremor so familiar to all dabblers in the psychic. Shortly thereafter it heaved slowly up and descended with a vast deliberation. There was a moment's stillness fraught with effort; then a rhythmic tap-tap-tap of one leg.

'Now,' said the doctor authoritatively. 'You will go into a trance, Mrs. Jarrett. Softly, easily. Let go. You're going into a trance. Going . . . going . . .' His voice was soothingly commanding.

Mrs. Jarrett moaned, her limbs jerked, she stretched as if in pain; then with a sigh she became inert.

'Watch out, Jimmy,' the doctor warned in a low voice. Then to the woman: 'Speak. Where are you? What do you see?'

The plump, limp bulk moaned again. The lips moved; inarticulate sounds proceeded from them, the fragments of unformed words; then a quivering sigh and silence. The doctor took occasion to lean first to one side and then to the other to listen to the breathing of Mr. Jarrett and the boy. Both were a little faster than normal; under the circumstances, not strange. With startling suddenness words cut the dark, clear and strong.

'I am in a place full of mist, I don't know where. Grey mist.' A laboured silence. Then: 'I am at the edge of something; something deep, dark.' A pause. 'Before me is a curtain, dim and misty—no—it seems—I think—no, it is the mist that is the curtain. There are dim things moving beyond the curtain.'

'Ha!' An exclamation of satisfaction from the doctor.

'I can't make them out. They are not animals; not people. They are dark things. Just—shapes.'

'Good God, that's what she said before!' The awed gasp was Mr. Jarrett's.

The sick man coughed gratingly.

'The shapes move, they twine and roll and swell up. They bulge up against the curtain as if to push through. It is dark; too dark on that side to see. I am afraid if one might push through ...'

Suddenly the boy whimpered, 'I don't like this. It's cold, an' I'm scared.'

The doctor could hear the hard breathing of Mr. Jarrett on his left as the table trembled under his sudden shiver. The doctor himself experienced an enveloping depression, an almost physical crawling of the cold hairs up and down his spine. The sick man went into a spasm of violent coughing.

Suddenly the voice screamed, 'One of the shapes is almost—my God, it *is* through! It's on this side. I can see—oh God, save me.'

'Lights, Jimmy!' snapped the doctor. 'Look to the sick man.'

The swift flood of illumination showed Mr. Jarrett grey and beaded with perspiration; the boy in wild-eyed terror; Terry, too, big-eyed, and nervously alert. All of them had felt a sudden stifling weight of a clutching fear that seemed to hang like a destroying wave about to break.

The sick man was in paroxysm of coughing from which he passed into a swoon of exhaustion. Only the woman had remained blissfully unconscious. The voice that had spoken out of her left her untroubled. In heavy peacefulness she slumped in her trance condition.

The doctor leaped round the table to her and placed his hands over her forehead in protection from he did not know exactly what. A chill still pervaded the room; a physical sense of cold and lifting of hair. Some enormous material menace had almost been able to swoop upon a victim. Slowly, with the flashing on of the lights, the horror faded.

The doctor bent over the unconscious lady. Smoothly he began to stroke her face, away from the centre towards her temples. As he stroked he talked, softly, reassuringly.

Presently the woman shuddered, heaved ponderously. Her eyes opened blankly, without comprehension. Wonder dawned in them at the confusion.

'I must have been asleep,' she murmured; and she was able to smile sheepishly. 'Tell me, did I—did my guides speak?'

That foolish, innocent question, coming from the only one in the room who knew nothing of what had happened, served to dissipate fear more than all the doctor's reassurances. The others began to take hold of themselves. The doctor was able to turn his attention to the sick man.

'How is his pulse, Jimmy? Hm-m, weak, but still going. He's just exhausted. That thing drew an awful lot of strength out of him. It nearly slipped one over on me; I didn't think it was through into this side yet.'

To his hosts he said with impressive gravity, 'It is necessary to tell you that we are faced with a situation that is more dangerous than I had thought. There is in this thing a distinct physical danger; it has gone beyond imagination and beyond "sensing" things. We are up against a malignant entity that is capable of human contacts. We must get the patient up to bed and then I shall try to explain what this danger is.'

He took the limp form in his arms with hardly an effort and signified to Mrs. Jarrett to lead the way. To all appearances it was no more than an unusually vigorous physician putting a patient to bed. But the doctor made one or two quite extraordinary innovations.

'Fresh air to the contrary,' he said grimly. 'Windows must remain shut and bolted. Let me see: iron catches are good. And, Johnny, you just run down to the kitchen and bring me up a fire iron—a poker, tongs, anything. A stove lid lifter will do.'

The boy clung to the close edges of the group. The doctor nodded with understanding.

'Mr. Jarrett, will you go? We mustn't leave our patient until we have him properly protected."

In a few moments Mr. Jarrett returned with a plain iron kitchen poker. That was just the thing, the doctor said. He placed it on the floor close along the door jamb. He herded the others out and, coming last himself, shut the door, pausing just a moment to note that the lock was of iron, after which he followed the wondering family down to the living-room. They sat expectant, uneasy.

'Now,' the doctor began, as though delivering a lecture. 'I want you all to listen carefully, because—I must tell you this, much as I dislike to frighten you—this thing has gone so far that a single mis-step may mean a death.'

He held up his hand. 'No, don't interrupt. I'm going to try to make clear what is difficult enough anyhow; and you must all try to understand it because an error now—even a little foolishness, a moment of forgetfulness—can open the way for a tragedy; because—now let me impress you with this—the thing that you have felt is a palpable force. I can tell you what it is, but I cannot tell you how it came to break into this side. This malignant force is'—he paused to weigh his words—'an elemental. I do not know how the thing was released. Maybe you had nothing to do with it. But you, madam'—to the trembling Mrs. Jarrett—'you caused it by playing with this seance business, about the dangers of which you know nothing. Nor have you taken the trouble even to read up on the subject. You have opened the way to attract this thing to your house; you and the unfortunate, innocent sick man upstairs. You've actually invited it to live among you.'

The faces of the audience expressed only fear of the unknown; fear and a blank lack of understanding. The doctor controlled his impatience and continued his lecture.

'I can't go into the complete theory of occultism here and now; but this much you must understand,' he said, pounding his fist on his knee for emphasis; 'It is an indubitable fact, known throughout the ages of human existence, and re-established by modern research, that there exist certain vast discarnate forces alongside of us and all around us. These forces function according to certain controlling laws, just as we do. They probably know as little about our laws as we do about theirs.

'There are many kinds of these forces. Forces of a high intelligence, far superior to ours; forces of possibly less intelligence; benevolent forces; malignant ones. They are all loosely generalized as spirits: elementals, subliminals, earthbounds and so on.

'These forces are separated from us, prevented from contact, by—what shall I say? I dislike the word, evil, or curtain; or, as the Bible puts it, the great gulf. They mean nothing. The best simile is perhaps in the modern invention of the radio.

'A certain set of wavelengths, ethereal vibrations, can impinge themselves upon a corresponding instrument attuned to those vibrations. A slight variation in wavelength, and the receiving instrument is a blank; totally unaffected, though it knows that vibrations of tremendous power exist all around it. It must tune in to become receptive to another set of vibrations.

'In something after this manner these discarnate so-called spirit forces are prevented from impinging themselves upon our consciousness. Sometimes we humans, for reasons of which we are very often unaware, do something, create a condition, which tunes us in with the vibration of a certain group of discarnate forces. Then we become conscious; we establish contact; we, in common parlance, see a ghost.'

The lecturer paused. Vague understanding was apparent on the faces of his fascinated audience.

'Good! Now then—I mentioned elementals. Elementals comprise one of these groups of discarnate forces; possibly the lowest of the group and the least intelligent. They have not evolved to human, or even animal form. They are just—shapes.'

'Oh, my God!' the shuddering moan came from Mrs. Jarrett. 'The shapes that I have sensed!'

'Exactly. You have sensed such a shape. Why have you sensed it? Because somehow, somewhere, something has happened that has enabled one of these elemental entities to tune in on the vibrations of our human wavelength, to break through the veil. What was the cause or how, we have no means of knowing. What we do know about elementals, as has been fully recognized by occultists of the past ages and has been pooh-poohed only by modern materialism, is that they are, to begin with, malignant; that is, hostile to human life. Then again—now mark this well—they can manifest themselves materially to humans only by drawing the necessary force from a human source, preferably from some human in a state of low resistance; from—a sick man.'

'Oh, my—my brother?' Mrs. Jarrett gasped her realization.

The doctor nodded slowly.

'Yes, his condition of low resistance and your thoughtless reaching for a contact in your seances have invited this malignant entity to this house. That is why the sick man has taken this sudden turn for the worse. The elemental is sapping his vitality in order to manifest itself materially. So far you have only felt its malevolent presence. Should it succeed in drawing to itself sufficient force it might be capable of enormous and destructive power. No, no, don't scream now; that doesn't help. You must all get a grip on yourselves so as calmly to take the proper defensive precautions.

'Fortunately we know an antidote; or let me say rather, a deterrent. Like most occult lore, this deterrent has been known and used by all peoples even up to this age of modern scepticism.

Savage people throughout the world use it; oriental peoples with a sensitivity keener than our own use it; modern white people use it, though unconsciously. The literature of magic is full of it.

'It is nothing more or less than iron. Cold iron. The iron nose-ring or toe-ring of the savage; the mantra loha of the Hindoos; the lucky horseshoe of your rural neighbours today. These things are not ornaments; they are amulets.

'We do not know why cold iron should act as a deterrent to certain kinds of hostile forces—call them spirits, if you like. But it is a fact known of old that a powerful antipathy exists between cold iron and certain of the lower orders of inhuman entities: doppelgangers, churels, incubi, wood runners, leperlings, and so on, and including all forms of elementals.

'So powerful is this antipathy that these hostile entities cannot approach a person or pass a passage so guarded. There are other forms of deterrents against some of the other discarnate entities: pentagons, Druid circles, etc., and even the holy water of the Church. Don't ask me why or how—perhaps it has something to do with molecular vibrations. Let us be glad, for the present, that we know of this deterrent. And let each of you go to bed now with a poker or a stove lid or whatever you fancy as an amulet, which I assure you will be ample to protect a normal healthy person who does not contrive to establish some special line of contact which may counteract the deterrent. In the case of the sick man I have taken the extra precaution of guarding even the door.

'Now the rest of you go to bed and *stay in your rooms*. If you're nervous, you may sleep all in one room. Dr. Terry and I will sit up and prowl around a bit. If you hear a noise it will be us doing night watchman. You can sleep in perfect security, unless you commit some piece of astounding foolishness which will open an unguarded avenue of contact. And one more thing: warn your brother, even if he should feel well enough, not in any circumstances to leave his room. Good night; and sleep well—if you can.'

Hesitant and unwilling the family went upstairs; huddled together, fearful of every new sound, every old shadow, not knowing how this horror that had come into the house might manifest itself; hating to go, but worn out by fatigue engendered of extreme terror.

'I'll bet they sleep all in one room like sardines,' commented the doctor.

Terry caught the note of anxiety and asked, 'Was that all the straight dope? I mean about elementals and so on? And iron? Sounds kind of foolish.'

The doctor's face was sober, the irises of his indeterminate eyes so pale that they were almost invisible in the artificial light.

'You never listened to a less foolish thing, my boy. It sounds so to you only because you have been bred in the school of modern materialism. What? Is it reasonable to maintain that we have during the last thin fringe of years on humanity's history obliterated what has been known to humanity ever since the first anthropoid hid his head under his hairy arms in terror? We have but pushed these things a little farther away; we have become less sensitive than our forefathers. And, having become less sensitive, we naturally do not inadvertently tune in on any other set of vibrations; and so we proclaim loudly that no such things exist. But we are beginning to learn again; and if you have followed the trend you will surely have noticed that many of our leading men of science, of thought, of letters, have admitted their belief in things which science and religion have tried to deny.'

Terry was impressed with the truth of his friend's statement. The possibilities thus opened up made him uneasy.

'Well, er-er, this—this elemental thing,' he said uneasily, 'can it do anything?'

'It can do'—the indeterminate eyes were far-away pin-points—'it can do anything, everything. Having once broken into our sphere, our plane, our wavelength—call it what you will—its malignant potentiality is measured only by the amount of force it can draw from its human source of supply. And remember—here is the danger of these things—the measure is not on a par ratio. It doesn't mean that such a malignant entity, drawing a few ounces of energy from a sick man, can exert only those few ounces. In some manner which we do not understand, all the discarnate intelligences know how to step-up an almost infinitesimal amount of human energy to many hundreds percent of power; as for instance the "spirits" that move heavy tables, perform levitation and so on. A malignant spirit can use that power as a deadly, destructive force.'

'But, good Lord,' burst out Terry, 'Why should the thing be malignant? Why, if it has broken through, got into tune with human vibrations, why should it want to destroy humans who have never done it any harm?'

The doctor did not reply at once. He was listening, alert and taut.

'Do these people keep a dog, do you know, Jimmy? Would that be it snuffling outside the door?'

But the noise, if there had been any, had ceased. The silence was sepulchral. The doctor relaxed and took up the last question.

'Why should it want to destroy life? That's something of a poser. I might say, how do I know? But I have a theory. Remember I said that elementals belonged to one of the least intelligent groups of discarnate entities. Now, the lower one goes in the scale of human intelligence, the more prevalent does one find the superstition that by killing one's enemy one acquires the good qualities of that enemy, his strength or his valour or his speed or something. In the lowest scale we find cannibalism, which is, as so many leading ethnologists have demonstrated, not a taste for human flesh, but a ceremony, a ritual whereby the eater absorbs the strength of the victim. And I suppose you know, incidentally, that militant modern atheists maintain that the holy communion is no other than a symbol of that very prevalent idea. An unintelligent elemental, then . . .'

The doctor suddenly gripped his friend's arm. A creak had sounded on the stairs. In the tense silence both men fancied they could detect a soft, sliding scuffle in that direction. With uncontrollable horror Terry's heart came up to his throat. In one panther bound the doctor reached the door and tore it open. Then he swore in baffled irritation.

Through the open door Terry could hear distinctly scurrying steps on the first landing. In sudden surge of horror at being left alone he leaped from his chair to follow his friend, and bumped into him at the door.

Dr. Muncing, cursing his luck in a most plebian manner, noted his expression and became immediately the scientist again.

'What's this, what's this? This won't do. Scare leaves you vulnerable. Now let me psychoanalyze you and eliminate that. Sit down and get this; it's quite simple and quite necessary before we start out chasing this thing. You feel afraid for two reasons. The first is psychological. Our forebears knew that certain aspects of the supernatural were genuinely fearsome. Unable to differentiate the superstition grew amongst the laity that all aspects were to be feared, just as most people fear all snakes, though only six per cent of them are poisonous. You have inherited both fear and superstition. Secondly, in this particular case, you sense the hostility of this thing and its potential power for destruction. Therefore, you are afraid.'

Under the doctor's cold logic, his friend was able to regain at least a grip on his emotions. With a smile he said, 'That's pretty thin comfort when even you admit its power for destruction.'

'*Potential*, I said. Don't forget, potential,' urged the doctor. 'It's power is capable of becoming enormous. Up to the present it has not been able to absorb very much energy. It evaded us just now instead of attacking us, and we have shut off its source of supply. Remember, too, its manifestation of itself must be physical. It may claw your hair in the dark; perhaps push you over the banisters if it gets a chance; but it can't sear your brain and blast your soul. It has drawn to itself sufficient physical energy to make itself heard; that means to be felt, and possibly to be seen. It has materialized; it cannot suddenly fade through walls and doors.'

'To be seen?' said Terry in awe-struck tones. 'Good gosh, what does a tangible hate look like?'

The doctor nodded. 'Well put, Jimmy; very well expressed. A tangible hate is just what this thing is. And since it is inherently a formless entity, a shape in the dark, manifesting itself by drawing upon human energy, it will probably look like some gross distortion of human form. Just malignant eyes, maybe, or clutching hands; or perhaps something more complete. Its object will be to skulk about the house seeking for an opening to absorb more energy to itself. Ours must be to rout it out.'

Mentally Terry was convinced. He could not fail to be, after that lucid exposition of exactly what they were up against. But physically the fine hair still rose on his spine. Shapeless things that could hate and could lurk in dark corners to trip one up on the stairs were sufficient reason for the very acme of human fear. However, he stood up. 'I'm with you,' he said shortly. 'Go ahead.'

The doctor held out his hand. 'Stout fellow. I knew you would, of course; and I brought this along for you as being quite the best weapon for this sort of a job. A blackjack in hand is a strong psychological bracer, and it has the virtue of being iron.'

Terry took the weighty little thing with a feeling of vast security, which was instantly dispelled by the doctor's next words.

'I suppose,' said Terry, 'That on account of the iron the thing can't approach one.'

'Don't fool yourself,' said the other. 'Iron is a deterrent. Not an absolute talisman in every case. We are going after this thing; we are *inviting* contact. Just as a savage dog may attack a man who is going after it with a club, so our desperate elemental, if it sees a chance, may—well, I don't know what it can do yet. Stick close, that's all.

Together the two men went up the stairs and stood in the upper hall. Four bedrooms and a bathroom opened off this. Two of the rooms they knew to be occupied. The other doors stood similarly closed.

'We've got to try the rooms,' the doctor whispered. 'It probably can, if necessary, open an unlocked door, though I doubt whether it would turn an iron key.'

Firmly, without hesitation, he opened one of the doors and stepped into the room. The doctor switched on the light. Nothing was to be seen, nothing heard, nothing felt.

'We'd sense it if it were here,' said the doctor as coolly as though hunting for nothing more tangible than an odour of escaping gas. 'It must be in the other empty room. Come on.'

He threw the door of that room wide open and stood, shoulder-to-shoulder with Terry, on the threshold. But there was nothing; no sound; no sensation.

'Queer,' muttered the doctor. 'It came up the stairs. It would hardly go into the bathroom, with an iron tub in it—though God knows, maybe cast iron molecules don't repel like hand-wrought metal.'

The bathroom drew blank. The two men looked at each other, and now Terry was able to grin. This matter of hunting for a presence that evaded them was not nearly so fearsome as his imagination had conjured up. The doctor's eyes narrowed to slits as he stood in thought.

'Another example,' he murmured, 'of the many truths in the Bible about the occult. Face the devil and he will fly from you, eh? I wonder where the devil this devil can be?'

As though in immediate answer came the rasping sounds of a dry grating cough.

Instinctively both men's heads flew round to face the sick man's door. But that remained undisturbed; the patient seemed to be sleeping soundly. Suddenly the doctor gripped his friend's arm and pointed—up to the ceiling.

'From the attic. See that trapdoor. It has taken on the cough with the vital energy it has been drawing from the sick man. I guess there'll be no lights up there. I'll go and get my flashlight. You stay here and guard the stairs. Then you can give me a boost up.'

The doctor was becoming more incredible every minute.

'You mean to say you propose to stick your head up through there?'

The doctor nodded soberly; his eyes were now black beads.

'It's quite necessary. You see, we've got to chase this thing out of the house while it is still weak, and then protect all entrances. Then, if it cannot quickly establish a contact with some other sick and non-resistant source of energy, it must go back to where it came from. Without a constant replenishment of human energy it can't keep up the human vibrations. That's the importance of shutting it out while it is still too weak to break through anybody else's resistance somewhere else. It's quite simple, isn't it? You sit tight and play cat over the mouse hole. I'll be right up again.'

Cat-like himself, the doctor ran down the steps. Terry felt chilled despite the fact that the hall was well lighted and he was armed. But that black square up there—if any cover belonged over it, it had been removed. The hole gaped dark, forbidding; and somewhere beyond it in the misty gloom a formless thing coughed consumptively. Terry, gazing at the hole in fascinated terror, imagined for himself a sudden framing of baleful eyes, a reaching down of a long taloned claw.

It grew to a horror, staring at that black opening, as into an evil world beyond. The effort of concentration became intolerable. Terry felt that he could not for the life of him hold his stare; he had to relieve himself of that tension or he would scream. He felt that cry welling up in his throat and the chill rising of hair on his scalp. He let his eyes drop and took a long breath to recover the control that was slipping from him.

There came a sharp click from the direction of the electric switch, and the hall was in sudden blackness.

Terry stood frozen, the cry choked in his throat. He could not tell how long he remained transfixed. An age passed in motionless fear of he did not know what. What had turned off the lights?

In the blackness a board creaked with awful deliberation. Terry could not tell where. His faculties refused to register. Only his wretched imagination—or was it his imagination?—conjured up a shadow, darker than the dark, poised on one grotesque foot like some monstrous misshapen carrion bird, watching him with a fell intentness. His pulse hammered at his temples for what seemed an eternity of horror. He computed time later by the fact that his eyes were becoming accustomed to the dim glow that came from the light downstairs.

Another board creaked, and now Terry felt his knees growing limp. But that was the doctor's firm step on the lower stairs. Terry's knees stiffened and he began to be able to breathe once more.

The shadow seemed to know that Dr. Muncing was returning, too. Terry was aware of a rush, of a dimly monstrous density of blackness that launched itself at him. He was hurled numbingly against the wall by a muffling air-cushion sort of impact. Helplessly dazed, smothered, he did not know how to resist, to defend himself. He was lost. And then the glutinous pressure recoiled, foiled. He could almost hear the baffled hate that withdrew from him and hurtled down the stairs.

His senses registered the fact that without his own volition he shouted, 'Look out!' and that there was a commotion somewhere below. He heard a stamping of feet and a surge of wind as though a window had been blasted open; and the next thing was the doctor's inquiry, 'Are you hurt?' and the beam of a flashlight racing up the steps.

He was not hurt; miraculously, it seemed to him, for the annihilating malevolence of that formless creature had appeared to be a vast force. But the doctor dressed him down severely.

'You lost your nerve, in spite of all that I explained to you. You let it influence your mind to fear and so played right into its hands. You laid yourself open to attack as smoothly as though you were Mrs. Jarrett herself. But out of that very evil we can draw the good of exemplary proof.

'You were helpless; paralyzed. And yet the thing drew off. Why? Because you had your iron blackjack in your hand. If it had known you had that defence it would never have attacked you, or it would have influenced you to put the iron down first. Knowing now that your have it, it will not, in its present condition of weakness, attack you again. So stick that in your hat and don't get panicky again. But we've got to keep after it. If we can keep it out of the house; if we can continue so to guard the sick man that the thing cannot draw any further energy from him its power to manifest itself must dwindle. We shall starve it out. And the more we can starve it, the less power will it have to break through the resistance of a new victim.'

'Come on, then,' said Terry.

'Good man,' approved the doctor. 'Come ahead. It went through the living-room window; that was the only one open. But, why, I ask myself. Why did it go out? That was just what we wanted it to do. I wonder whether it is up to some devilish trick. The thing can think with a certain animal cunning. We must shut and lock the living-room window and go out at the door. What trick has that thing in store, I wonder? What damnable trick?'

'How are we going to find an abstract hate in this maze of shadows?' Terry wanted to know.

'It is more than abstract,' said the doctor seriously. 'Having broken into our plane of existence, this thing has achieved, as you have already felt, a certain state of semi-materialization. A ponderable substance has formed round the nucleus of malignant intelligence. As long as it can draw upon human energy from its victim, that material substance will remain. In moving from place to place, it must make a certain amount of noise. And, drawing its physical energy from this particular sick man, it must cough as he does. In a good light, even in this bright moonlight, it will be, to a certain extent, visible.'

But no rustlings and scurryings fled before their flashlights amongst the ornamental evergreens; no furtive shadow flitted across moonlight patches; no sense of hate hung in the darkest corners.

'I hope to God it didn't give us the slip and sneak in again before we got the entries fixed. But no, I'm sure it wasn't in the house. I wish I could guess what tricks it's up to.' The doctor was more worried than he cared to let his friend see. He was convinced that leaving the house had been a deliberate move on the thing's part and he wished that he might fathom whatever cunning purpose lay back of that move.

All of a sudden the sound of footsteps impinged upon their ears; faint shuffling. Both men tensed to listen, and they could hear the steps coming nearer. The doctor shook his head.

'It's just some countryman trudging home along the road. If he sees us with flashlights at this hour he'll raise a howl of burglars, no doubt.'

The footsteps approached ploddingly behind the fence, one of those nine-foot high ornamental screens made of split chestnut saplings that are so prevalent around country houses. Presently the dark figure of the man—Terry was quite relieved to see that it was a man—passed before the open gate, and the footsteps trudged on behind the tall barrier.

Fifty feet, a hundred feet; the crunch of heavy nailed boots was growing fainter. Then something rustled amongst the bushes. Terry caught at the doctor's sleeve. 'There! My God! There again!'

A crouching something ran with incredible speed along this side of the fence after the unsuspecting footsteps of the other. In the patches of moonlight between black shadows it was easily distinguishable. It came abreast with the retreating footsteps and suddenly it jumped. Without preparation or take-off, apparently without effort, the swiftly scuttling thing shot itself into the air.

Both men saw a ragged-edged form, as that of an incredibly tall and thin man with an abnormally tiny head, clear the nine-foot fence with bony knees drawn high and attenuated ape arms flung wide; an opium eater's nightmare silhouetted against the dim sky. And then it was gone.

In the instant that they stood rooted to the spot, a shriek of inarticulate terror rose from the road. There was a spurt of flying gravel, a mad plunging of racing footsteps, more shrieks, the last rising to the high-pitched falsetto of the acme of fear. Then a lurching fall and an awful silence.

'Good God!' The doctor was racing for the gate, Terry after him. A hundred feet down the road a dark mass huddled on the ground; there was not a sign of anything else. The misshapen shadow had vanished. The man on the ground rolled limp, giving vent to great gulping moans. The doctor lifted his shoulders against his own knee.

'Keep a look-out, Jimmy,' he warned. His deft hands were exploring for a hurt or wound, while his rapid fire of comments gave voice to his findings. 'What damned luck! Still, I don't see what it could have done to a sturdy lout like this. How could we have guarded against this sort of a mischance? Though it just couldn't have crashed into this fellow's vitality so suddenly; there doesn't seem to be anything wrong, anyhow. I guess he's more scared than hurt.'

The moaning hulk of a man squirmed and opened his eyes. Feeling himself in the grip of hands, he let out another fearful yell and struggled in a frenzy to escape.

'Easy, brother, easy,' the doctor said soothingly. 'You're all right. Get a hold of yourself.'

The man shuddered convulsively. Words babbled from his sagging lips. 'It-it-its ha-hand! Oh, G—God—over my face. A h-hand like an eel—a dead ee-eel. Ee-ee!'

He went off into a high-pitched hysteria again.

There was a sound of windows opening up at the house and a confused murmur of anxious voices; then a hail.

'What is it? Who's there? What's the matter?'

'Lord help the fools!' The doctor dropped the man cold in the road and sprang across to the other side from where he could look over the high fence and see the square of patches of light from the windows high up on their little hill.

'Back!' he screamed. 'Get back! For God's sake, shut those windows!' He waved his hands and jumped down in an agony of apprehension. 'What?' The fatuous query floated down to him. 'What's that you say?'

Another square of light suddenly sprang out of the looming mass, from the sick man's room. Laboriously the window went up, and the sick man leaned out.

'What?' he asked, and he coughed out into the night.

'God Almighty! Come on, Jimmy! Leave that fool; he's only scared.' The doctor shouted and dashed off on the long sprint back to the gate and up the sloping shrubbery to the house that he had thought to leave so well guarded.

'That's its trick,' he panted as he ran. 'That's why it came out. Please Providence we won't come too late. But it's got the start on us, and it can move ten times as fast.'

Together they burst through the front door, slammed it after them, and thundered up the stairs. The white, owlish faces of the Jarrett family gleamed palely at them from their door. The doctor cursed them for fools as he dashed past. He tore at the knob of the sick-room door.

The door did not budge.

Frantically he wrestled with it. It held desperately solid.

'Bolted from the inside!' The doctor screamed. 'The fool must have done it himself. Open up in there. Quick! Open for your life.'

The door remained cold and dead. Only from inside the room came the familiar hacking cough. It came in a choking fit. And then Terry's blood ebbed in a chill wave right down to his feet.

For *there were two coughs*. A ghastly chorus of rasping and retching in a hell's paroxysm.

The doctor ran back the length of the hall. Pushing off from the further wall, he dashed across and crashed his big shoulders against the door. Like petty nails the bolt screws flew and he staggered in, clutching the sagging door for support.

The room was in heavy darkness. The doctor clawed wildly along the wall for the unfamiliar light switch. Terry, at his heels, felt the wave of malevolence that met them.

The sudden light revealed to their blinking eyes the sick man, limp, inert, lying where he had been hurled, half in and half out of the bed, twisted in a horrible paroxysm.

The window was open, as the wretched dupe had left it when he poked his foolish head out into the night to inquire about all the hubbub outside. Above the corner of the sill, hanging outside, was a horror that drew both men up short. An abnormally long angle of raggy elbow supported a smudgy, formless, yellow face of incredible evil that grinned malignant triumph out of an absurdly infantile head.

The face dropped out of sight. Only hate, like a tangible thing, pervaded the room. From twenty feet below came back to the trembling men a grating, 'Och-och-och, ha-ha-ha-heh-heh-heck, och—och.' It retreated down the shrubbery.

Dr. Muncing stood a long minute in choked silence. Then bitterly he swore. Slowly, with incisive grimness he said, 'Man's ingenuity can guard against everything except the sheer dumb stupidity of man.'

It was morning. Dr. Muncing was taking his leave. He was leaving behind him a few last words of advice. They were not gentle.

'I shall say no more about the criminal stupidity of opening your windows after my warning to you; perhaps the thing was able to influence all of you. Your brother, madam, has paid the price.

Through your fault and his, there is now loose, somewhere in our world, an elemental entity, malignant and having sufficient human energy to continue. Where or how, I cannot say. It may turn up in the next town, it may do so in China; or something may happen to dissipate it.

'As far as you are concerned it is through. It has tapped this source of energy and has gone on. It will not come back, unless you, madam, go out of your way deliberately to attract it by fooling with these silly seances before you have learned a lot more about them than you know now.'

Mrs. Jarrett was penitent and very wholesomely frightened, besides. She would never play with fire again, she vowed; she would have nothing at all to do with it ever again; she would be glad if the doctor would take away her ouija board and her planchette and all her notebooks; everything. She was afraid of them; she felt that some horrible influence still attached to them.

'Notebooks?' The doctor was interested. 'You mean you took notes of the babble that came through? Let me see. Hm-m, the usual stuff; projected reversal of your own conceptions of the hereafter and how happy all your relatives are there. Ha, what's this? Numbers, numbers—twelve, twenty-four, eight—all the bad combinations of numbers. What perversity made you think only of bad numbers? Hello, hello, what—From where did you get this recurring ten, five, eight, one, fourteen? A whole page of it. And here again. And here; eighteen, one, ten? Pages and pages—and a lot of worse ones here? How did this come?'

Mrs. Jarrett was tearful and appeared somewhat hesitant.

'They just came through like that, Doctor. They kept on coming. We just wrote them down.'

The doctor was very serious. A thin whistle formed in his pursed lips. His eyes were dark pools of wonder.

'There are more things in heaven and earth—' He muttered. Then shaking off the awe that had come over him, he turned to Mrs. Jarrett.

'My dear lady,' he said. 'I apologize about those open windows. This thing was able to project its influence from even the other side of the veil. *It made you invite it*. Don't ask me to explain these mysteries. But listen to what you have been playing with.' The doctor paused to let his words soak in.

'These numbers, translated into their respective letters, are the beginning of an ancient *Hindoo Yogi spell to invoke a devil*. Merciful heaven, how many things we don't understand. So that's how it came through. And there is no Yogi spell to send it back. We shall probably meet again, that thing and I.'

THE SALEM MASS

Nathaniel Hawthorne

*

Young Goodman Brown came forth at sunset into the street of Salem village; but put his head back, after crossing the threshold, to exchange a parting kiss with his young wife. And Faith, as the wife was aptly named, thrust her own pretty head into the street, letting the wind play with the pink ribbons of her cap while she called to Goodman Brown.

'Dearest heart,' whispered she, softly and rather sadly, when her lips were close to his ear, 'prithee put off your journey until sunrise and sleep in your own bed tonight. A lone woman is troubled with such dreams and such thoughts that she's afeared of herself sometimes. Pray tarry with me this night, dear husband, of all nights in the year.'

'My love and my Faith,' replied young Goodman Brown, 'of all nights in the year, this one must I tarry away from thee. My journey, as thou callest it, forth and back again, must needs be done 'twixt now and sunrise. What, my sweet, pretty wife, dost thou doubt me already, and we but three months married?'

'Then God bless you!' said Faith, with pink ribbons; 'and may you find all well when you come back.'

'Amen!' cried Goodman Brown. 'Say thy prayers, dear Faith, and go to bed at dusk, and no harm will come to thee.'

So they parted; and the young man pursued his way until, being about to turn the corner by the meeting-house, he looked back and saw the head of Faith still peeping after him with a melancholy air, in spite of her pink ribbons.

'Poor little Faith!' thought he, for his heart smote him. 'What a wretch am I to leave her on such an errand! She talks of dreams, too. Methought as she spoke, there was trouble in her face, as if a dream had warned her what work is to be done tonight. But no, no; 'twould kill her to think it. Well, she's a blessed angel on earth; and after this one night I'll cling to her skirts and follow her to heaven.'

With this excellent resolve for the future, Goodman Brown felt himself justified in making more haste on his present evil purpose. He had taken a dreary road, darkened by all the gloomiest trees of the forest, which barely stood aside to let the narrow path creep through, and closed immediately behind. It was all as lonely as could be; and there is this peculiarity in such a solitude, that the traveller knows not who may be concealed by the innumerable trunks and the thick boughs overhead; so that with lonely footsteps he may yet be passing through an unseen multitude.

'There may be a devilish Indian behind every tree,' said Goodman Brown to himself; and he glanced fearfully behind him as he added, 'What if the Devil himself should be at my very elbow!'

His head being turned back, he passed a crook of the road, and, looking forward again, beheld the figure of a man, in grave and decent attire, seated at the foot of an old tree. He arose at Goodman Brown's approach and walked onward side by side with him.

'You are late, Goodman Brown,' said he. 'The clock of the Old South was striking as I came through Boston; and that is full fifteen minutes agone.'

'Faith kept me back awhile,' replied the young man, with a

tremor in his voice, caused by the sudden appearance of his companion, though not wholly unexpected.

It was now deep dusk in the forest, and deepest in that part of it where these two were journeying. As nearly as could be discerned, the second traveller was about fifty years old, apparently in the same rank of life as Goodman Brown, and bearing a considerable resemblance to him, though perhaps more in expression than features. Still they might have been taken for father and son. And yet, though the elder person was as simply clad as the younger and as simple in manner too, he had an indescribable air of one who knew the world, and who would not have felt abashed at the governor's dinner-table or in King William's court, were it possible that his affairs should call him thither. But the only thing about him that could be fixed upon as remarkable was his staff, which bore the likeness of a great black snake, so curiously wrought that it might almost be seen to twist and wriggle itself like a living serpent. This, of course, must have been an ocular deception, assisted by the uncertain light.

'Come, Goodman Brown,' cried his fellow-traveller, 'this is a dull pace for the beginning of a journey. Take my staff, if you are so soon weary.'

'Friend,' said the other, exchanging his slow pace for a full stop, 'having kept covenant by meeting thee here, it is my purpose now to return when I came. I have scruples touching the matter thou wot'st of.'

'Sayest thou so?' replied he of the serpent, smiling apart. 'Let us walk on, nevertheless, reasoning as we go; and if I convince thee not, thou shalt turn back. We are but a little way in the forest yet.'

'Too far! too far!' exclaimed the good man, unconsciously resuming his walk. 'My father never went into the woods on such an errand, nor his father before him. We have been a race of honest men and good Christians since the days of the martyrs; and shall I be the first by the name of Brown that ever took this path and kept – '

'Such company, thou wouldn't say,' observed the elder person, interpreting his pause. 'Well said, Goodman Brown! I have been as well acquainted with your family as with ever a one among the Puritans; and that's no trifle to say. I helped your grandfather, the constable, when he lashed the Quaker woman so smartly through the streets of Salem; and it was I that brought your father a pitch-pine knot, kindled at my own hearth, to set fire to an Indian village, in King Philip's war. They were my good friends both; and many a pleasant walk have we had along this path, and returned merrily after midnight. I would fain be friends with you for their sake.'

'If it be as thou sayest,' replied Goodman Brown, 'I marvel they never spoke of these matters; or, verily, I marvel not, seeing that the least rumour of the sort would have driven them from New England. We are a people of prayer, and good works to boot, and abide no such wickedness.'

'Wickedness or not,' said the traveller with the twisted staff, 'I have a very general acquaintance here in New England. The deacons of divers towns make me their chairman; and a majority of the Great and General Court are firm supporters of my interests. The governor and I, too – these are state secrets.'

'Can this be so?' cried Goodman Brown, with a stare of amazement at his undisturbed companion. 'Howbeit, I have nothing to do with the governor and council; they have their own ways, and are no rule for a simple husbandman like me. But, were I to go on with thee, how should I meet the eye of that good old man, our minister, at Salem village? Oh, his voice would make me tremble both Sabbath day and lecture day!'

Thus far the elder traveller had listened with due gravity; but now burst into a fit of irrepressible mirth, shaking himself so violently that his snake-like staff actually seemed to wriggle in sympathy.

'Ha! ha! ha!' shouted he again and again; then composing himself, 'Well, go on, Goodman Brown, go on; but, prithee, don't kill me with laughing.'

'Well, then, to end the matter at once,' said Goodman Brown, considerably nettled, 'there is my wife, Faith. It would break her dear little heart, and I'd rather break my own.'

'Nay, if that be the case,' answered the other, 'e'en go thy ways, Goodman Brown. I would not for twenty old women like the one hobbling before us that Faith should come to any harm.'

As he spoke, he pointed his staff at a female figure on the path, in whom Goodman Brown recognised a very pious and exemplary dame, who had taught him catechism in youth, and was still his moral and spiritual adviser, jointly with the minister and Deacon Gookin.

'A marvel, truly, that Goody Cloyse should be so far in the

wilderness at nightfall,' said he. 'But, with your leave, friend, I shall take a cut through the woods until we have left this Christian woman behind. Being a stranger to you, she might ask whom I was consorting with and whither I was going.'

'Be it so,' said his fellow-traveller. 'Betake you to the woods, and let me keep the path.'

Accordingly the young man turned aside, but took care to watch his companion, who advanced softly along the road until he had come within a staff's length of the old dame. She, meanwhile, was making the best of her way, with singular speed for so aged a woman, and mumbling some indistinct words – a prayer, doubtless – as she went. The traveller put forth his staff and touched her withered neck with what seemed the serpent's tail.

'The Devil!' screamed the pious old lady.

'Then Goody Cloyse knows her old friend?' observed the traveller, confronting her and leaning on his writhing stick.

'Ah, forsooth, and is it your worship indeed?' cried the good old dame. 'Yea, truly it is, and in the very image of my old gossip, Goodman Brown, the grandfather of the silly fellow that now is. But – would your worship believe it? – my broomstick hath strangely disappeared, stolen as I suspect, by that unhanged witch, Goody Cory, and that, too, when I was all anointed with the juice of smallage, and cinquefoil, and wolf's-bane –'

'Mingled with fine wheat and the fat of a new-born babe,' said the shape of old Goodman Brown.

'Ah, your worship knows the recipe,' cried the old lady, cackling aloud. 'So, as I was saying, being all ready for the meeting, and no horse to ride on, I made up my mind to foot it; for they tell me there is a nice young man to be taken into communion tonight. But now your good worship will lend me your arm, and we shall be there in a twinkling.'

'That can hardly be,' answered her friend. 'I may not spare you my arm, Goody Cloyse; but here is my staff, if you will.'

So saying, he threw it down at her feet, where, perhaps, it assumed life, being one of the rods which its owner had formerly lent to the Egyptian magi. Of this fact, however, Goodman Brown could not take cognizance. He had cast up his eyes in astonishment, and looking down again, beheld neither Goody Cloyse nor the serpentine staff, but his fellow-traveller alone, who waited for him as calmly as if nothing had happened.

'That old woman taught me my catechism,' said the young man; and there is a world of meaning in this simple comment.

They continued to walk onward, while the elder traveller exhorted his companion to make good speed and persevere in the path, discoursing so aptly that his arguments seemed rather to spring up in the bosom of his auditor than to be suggested by himself. As they went, he plucked a branch of maple to serve for a walking-stick, and began to strip it of the twigs and little boughs, which were wet with evening dew. The moment his fingers touched them they became strangely withered and dried up as with a week's sunshine. Thus the pair proceeded, at a good free pace, until suddenly, in a gloomy hollow of the road Goodman Brown sat himself down on the stump of a tree and refused to go any farther.

'Friend,' said he, stubbornly, 'my mind is made up. Not another step will I budge on this errand. What if a wretched old woman do choose to go to the Devil when I thought she was going to heaven: is that any reason why I should quit my dear Faith and go after her?'

'You will think better of this by and by,' said his acquaintance, composedly. 'Sit here and rest yourself awhile; and when you feel like moving again, there's my staff to help you along.'

Without more words, he threw his companion the maple stick, and was as speedily out of sight as if he had vanished into the deepening gloom. The young man sat a few moments by the roadside, applauding himself greatly and thinking with how clear a conscience he should meet the minister in his morning walk, nor shrink from the eye of good old Deacon Gookin. And what calm sleep would be his that very night, which was to have been spent so wickedly, but so purely and sweetly now, in the arms of Faith! Amidst these pleasant and praiseworthy meditations, Goodman Brown heard the tramp of horses along the road, and deemed it advisable to conceal himself within the verge of the forest, conscious of the guilty purpose that had brought him thither, though now so happily turned from it.

On came the hoof-tramps and the voices of the riders, two grave old voices, conversing soberly as they drew near. These mingled sounds appeared to pass along the road, within a few yards of the young man's hiding-place; but, owing doubtless to the depth of the gloom at that particular spot, neither the travellers nor their steeds were visible. Though their figures brushed the small boughs by the wayside, it could not be seen that they intercepted, even for a moment, the faint gleam from the strip of bright sky athwart which they must have passed. Goodman Brown alternately crouched and stood on tiptoe, pulling aside the branches and thrusting forth his head as far as he durst, without discerning so much as a shadow. It vexed him the more, because he could have sworn, were such a thing possible, that he recognised the voices of the minister and Deacon Gookin, jogging along quietly, as they were wont to do, when bound to some ordination or ecclesiastical council. While yet within hearing, one the riders stopped to pluck a switch.

'Of the two, reverend sir,' said the voice like the deacon's, 'I had rather miss an ordination dinner than tonight's meeting. They tell me that some of our community are to be here from Falmouth and beyond, and others from Connecticut and Rhode Island, besides several of the Indian pow-wows, who, after their fashion, know almost as much devilry as the best of us. Moreover, there is a goodly young woman to be taken into communion.'

'Mighty well, Deacon Gookin!' replied the solemn old tones of the minister. 'Spur up, or we shall be late. Nothing can be done, you know, until I get on the ground.'

The hoofs clattered again; and the voices, talking so strangely in the empty air, passed on through the forest, where no church had ever been gathered or solitary Christian prayed. Whither, then, could these holy men be journeying so deep into the heathen wilderness? Young Goodman Brown caught hold of a tree for support, being ready to sink down on the ground, faint and overburdened with the heavy sickness of his heart. He looked up to the sky, doubting whether there really was a heaven above him. Yet there was the blue arch, and the stars brightening in it.

'With heaven above and Faith below, I will yet stand firm against the Devil!' cried Goodman Brown.

While he still gazed upward into the deep arch of the firmament and had lifted his hands to pray, a cloud, though no wind was stirring, hurried across the zenith and hid the brightening stars. The blue sky was still except directly overhead, where this black mass of cloud was sweeping swiftly northward. Aloft in the air, as if from the depths of the cloud, came a confused and doubtful sound of voices. Once the listener fancied that he could distinguish the accents of townspeople of his own, men and women, both pious and ungodly, many of whom he had met at the communion-table, and had seen others rioting at the tavern. The next moment, so indistinct were the sounds, he doubted whether he had heard aught but the murmur of the old forest, whispering without a wind. Then came a stronger swell of those familiar tones, heard daily in the sunshine at Salem village, but never until now from a cloud of night. There was one voice, of a young woman, uttering lamentations, yet with an uncertain sorrow, and entreating for some favour, which, perhaps, it would grieve her to obtain; and all the unseen multitudes, both saints and sinners, seemed to encourage her onward.

'Faith!' shouted Goodman Brown, in a voice of agony and desperation; and the echoes of the forest mocked him, crying, 'Faith! Faith!' as if bewildered wretches were seeking her all through the wilderness.

The cry of grief, rage and terror was yet piercing the night, when the unhappy husband held his breath for a response. There was a scream, drowned immediately in a louder murmur of voices, fading into far-off laughter, as the dark cloud swept away, leaving the clear and silent sky above Goodman Brown. But something fluttered lightly down through the air and caught on the branch of a tree. The young man seized it, and beheld a pink ribbon.

'My Faith is gone!' cried he, after one stupefied moment. 'There is no good on earth; and sin is but a name. Come, Devil; for to thee is this world given.'

And, maddened with despair, so that he laughed aloud and long, did Goodman Brown grasp his staff and set forth again, at such a rate that he seemed to fly along the forest path rather than to walk or run. The road grew wilder and drearier and more faintly traced, and vanished at length, leaving him in the heart of the dark wilderness, still rushing onward with the instinct that guides mortal man to evil. The whole forest was peopled with frightful sounds – the creaking of the trees, the howling of wild beasts, and the yell of Indians; while sometimes the wind tolled like a distant church -bell,and sometimes gave a broad roar around the traveller, as if all Nature were laughing him to scorn. But he was himself the chief horror of the scene, and shrank not from its other horrors.

'Ha! ha! ha!' roared Goodman Brown when the wind laughed at him. 'Let us hear which will laugh loudest. Think not to frighten me with your devilry. Come witch, come wizard, come Indian pow-wow, come Devil himself, and here comes Goodman Brown. You may as well fear him as he fear you.'

In truth, all through the haunted forest there could be nothing more frightful than the figure of Goodman Brown. On he flew among the black pines, brandishing his staff with frenzied gestures, now giving vent to an inspiration of horrid blasphemy, and now shouting forth such laughter as set all the echoes of the forest laughing like demons around him. The fiend in his own shape is less hideous than when he rages in the breast of man. Thus sped the demoniac on his course, until, quivering among the trees, he saw a red light before him, as when the felled trunks and branches of a clearing have been set on fire, and throw up their lurid blaze against the sky, at the hour of midnight. He paused, in a lull of the tempest that had driven him onward, and heard the swell of what seemed a hymn rolling solemnly from a distance with the weight of many voices. He knew the tune; it was a familiar one in the choir of the village meeting-house. The verse died heavily away, and was lengthened by a chorus, not of human voices, but of all the sounds of the benighted wilderness pealing in awful harmony together. Goodman Brown cried out; and his cry was lost to his own ear by its unison with the cry of the desert.

In the interval of silence he stole forward until the light glared full upon his eyes. At one extremity of an open space, hemmed in by the dark wall of the forest, arose a rock, bearing some rude, natural resemblance either to an altar or a pulpit and surrounded by four blazing pines, their tops aflame, their stems untouched, like candles at an evening meeting. The mass of foliage that had overgrown the summit of the rock was all on fire, blazing high into the night and fitfully illuminating the whole field. Each pendent twig and leafy festoon was in a blaze. As the red light arose and fell, a numerous congregation alternately shone forth, then disappeared in shadow, and again grew, as it were, out of the darkness, peopling the heart of the solitary woods at once.

'A grave and dark-clad company,' quoth Goodman Brown. In truth they were such. Among them, quivering to and fro between gloom and splendour, appeared faces that would be seen next day at the council board of the province, and others which, Sabbath after Sabbath, looked devoutly heavenward, and benignantly over the crowded pews, from the holiest pulpits in the land. Some affirmed that the lady of the governor was there. At least there were high dames well known to her, and wives of honoured husbands, and widows, a great multitude, and ancient maidens, all of excellent repute, and fair young girls, who trembled lest their mothers should espy them. Either the sudden gleams of light flashing over the obscure field bedazzled Goodman Brown, or he recognised a score of the church members of Salem village famous for their especial sanctity. Good old Deacon Gookin had arrived, and waited at the skirts of that venerable saint, his reverend pastor. But, irreverently consorting with these grave, reputable, and pious people, these elders of the church, these chaste dames and dewy virgins, there were men of dissolute lives and women of spotted fame, wretches given over to all mean and filthy vice and suspected even of horrid crimes. It was strange to see that the good shrank not from the wicked, nor were the sinners abashed by the saints. Scattered also among their pale-faced enemies were the Indian priests, or pow-wows, who had often scared their native forest with more hideous incantations than any known to English witchcraft.

'But where is Faith?' thought Goodman Brown; and, as hope came into his heart, he trembled.

Another verse of the hymn arose, a slow and mournful strain, such as the pious love, but joined to words which expressed all that our nature can conceive of sin, and darkly hinted at far more. Unfathomable to mere mortals is the lore of fiends. Verse after verse was sung; and still the chorus of the desert swelled between like the deepest tone of a mighty organ; and with the final peal of that dreadful anthem there came a sound, as if the roaring wind, the rushing streams, the howling beasts, and every other voice of the unconverted wilderness were mingling and according with the voice of guilty man in homage to the prince of all. The four blazing pines threw up a loftier flame, and obscurely discovered shapes and visages of horror on the smoke wreaths above the impious assembly. At the same moment the fire on the rock shot redly forth and formed a glowing arch above its base, where now appeared a figure. With reverence be it spoken, the figure bore no slight similitude, both in garb and manner, to some grave divine of the New England churches.

'Bring forth the converts!' cried a voice that echoed through the field and rolled into the forest.

At the word, Goodman Brown stepped forth from the shadow of the trees and approached the congregation, with whom he felt a loathful brotherhood by the sympathy of all that was wicked in his heart. He could have wellnigh sworn that the shape of his own dead father beckoned him to advance, looking downward from a smoke-wreath, while a woman, with dim features of despair, threw out her hand to warn him back. Was it his mother? But he had no power to retreat one step, nor to resist, even in thought, when the minister and good old Deacon Gookin seized his arms and led him to the blazing rock. Thither came also the slender form of a veiled female, led between Goody Cloyse, that pious teacher of the catechism, and Martha Carrier, who had received the Devil's promise to be queen of hell. A rampant hag was she. And there stood the proselytes beneath the canopy of fire.

'Welcome my children,' said the dark figure, 'to the communion of your race. Ye have found thus young your nature and your destiny. My children, look behind you!'

They turned; and flashing forth, as it were, in a sheet of flame, the fiend worshippers were seen; the smile of welcome gleamed darkly on every visage.

'There,' resumed the sable form, 'are all whom ye have reverenced from youth. Ye deemed them holier than yourselves, and shrank from your own sin, contrasting it with their lives of righteousness and prayful aspirations heavenwards. Yet here are they all in my worshipping assembly. This night it shall be granted to you to know their secret deeds; how hoary-bearded elders of the church have whispered wanton words to the young maids of their households; how many a woman, eager for widow's weeds, has given her husband a drink at bedtime and let him sleep his last sleep in her bosom; how beardless youths have made haste to inherit their father's wealth; and how fair damsels – blush not, sweet ones – have dug little graves in the garden and bidden me, the sole guest, to an infant's funeral. By the sympathy of your human hearts for sin ye shall scent out all the places – whether in church, bedchamber, street, field or forest – where crime has been commited, and shall exult to behold the whole earth one stain of guilt, one mighty blood-spot. Far more than this. It shall be yours to penetrate, in every bosom, the deep mystery of sin, the fountain of all wicked arts, and which inexhaustibly supplies more evil impulses than human power – than my power at its utmost – can make manifest in deeds. And now, my children, look upon each other.'

They did so; and, by the blaze of the hell-kindled torches, the wretched man beheld his Faith, and the wife her husband, trembling before that unhallowed altar.

'Lo, there ye stand, my children,' said the figure, in a deep and solemn tone, almost sad with its despairing awfulness, as if his once angelic nature could yet mourn for our miserable race. 'Depending upon one another's hearts, ye had still hoped that virtue were not all a dream. Now are ye undeceived. Evil is the nature of mankind. Evil must be your only happiness. Welcome again, my children, to the communion of your race.'

'Welcome,' repeated the fiend worshippers, in one cry of despair and triumph.

And there they stood, the only pair, as it seemed, who were yet hesitating on the verge of wickedness in this dark world. A basin was hollowed, naturally, in the rock. Did it contain water, reddened by the lurid light? or was it blood? or, perchance, a liquid flame? Herein did the shape of evil dip his hand and prepare to lay the mark of baptism upon their foreheads, that they might be partakers of the mystery of sin, more conscious of the secret guilt of others, both in deed and thought than they could now be of their own. The husband cast one look at his pale wife, and Faith at him. What polluted wretches would the next glance show them to each other, shuddering alike at what they disclosed and what they saw!

'Faith! Faith!' cried the husband, 'look up to Heaven, and resist the wicked one.'

Whether Faith obeyed, he knew not. Hardly had he spoken, when he found himself amid calm night and solitude, listening to a roar of the wind which died heavily away through the forest. He staggered against the rock, and felt it chill and damp; while a hanging twig, that had been all on fire, besprinkled his cheek with the coldest dew.

The next morning young Goodman Brown came slowly into the street of Salem village, staring around him like a bewildered man. The good old minister was taking a walk along the graveyard to get an appetite for breakfast and meditate his sermon and bestowed a blessing, as he passed, on Goodman Brown. He shrank from the venerable saint as if to avoid an anathema. Old Deacon Gookin was at domestic worship, and the holy words of his prayer were heard through the open window. 'What God doth the wizard pray to?' quoth Goodman Brown. Goody Cloyse, that excellent old Christian, stood in the early sunshine at her own lattice, catechizing a little girl who had brought her a pint of morning's milk. Goodman Brown snatched away the child as from the grasp of the fiend himself. Turning the corner by the meeting-house, he spied the head of

Faith, with the pink ribbons, gazing anxiously forth, and bursting into such joy at sight of him that she skipped along the street and almost kissed her husband before the whole village. But Goodman Brown looked sternly and sadly into her face, and passed on without a greeting.

Had Goodman Brown fallen asleep in the forest, and only dreamed a wild dream of a witch-meeting?

Be it so, if you will; but, alas! it was a dream of evil omen for young Goodman Brown. A stern, a sad, a darkly meditative, a distrustful, if not a desperate, man did he become from the night of that fearful dream. On the Sabbath day, when the congregation were singing a holy psalm, he could not listen, because the anthem of sin rushed loudly upon his ear and drowned all the blessed strain. When the minister spoke from the pulpit, with power and fervid eloquence, and with his hand on the open Bible, of the sacred truths of our religion, and of saint-like lives and triumphant deaths, and of future bliss or misery unutterable, then did Goodman Brown turn pale, dreading lest the roof should thunder down upon the grey blasphemer and his hearers. Often, awakening suddenly at midnight, he shrank from the bosom of Faith; and at morning or eventide, when the family knelt down to prayer, he scowled, and muttered to himself, and gazed sternly at his wife, and turned away. And when he had lived long, and was borne to his grave, a hoary corpse, followed by Faith, an aged woman, and children and grand-children, a goodly procession, besides neighbours not a few, they carved no hopeful verse upon his tombstone; for his dying hour was gloom.

Witches' Hollow

H. P. LOVECRAFT

District School Number Seven stood on the very edge of that wild country which lies west of Arkham. It stood in a little grove of trees, chiefly oaks and elms with one or two maples; in one direction the road led to Arkham, in the other it dwindled away into the wild, wooded country which always looms darkly on that western horizon. It presented a warmly attractive appearance to me when first I saw it on my arrival as the new teacher early in September, 1920, though it had no distinguishing architectural feature and was in every respect the replica of thousands of country schools scattered throughout New England, a compact, conservative building painted white, so that it shone forth from among the trees in the midst of which it stood.

It was an old building at that time, and no doubt has since been abandoned or torn down. The school district has now been consolidated, but at that time it supported this school in somewhat niggardly a manner, skimping and saving on every necessity. Its standard readers, when I came there to teach, were still *McGuffey's Eclectic Readers,* in editions published before the turn of the century. My charges added up to twenty-seven. There were Allens and Whateleys and Perkinses, Dunlocks and Abbotts and Talbots—and there was Andrew Potter.

I cannot now recall the precise circumstances of my especial notice of Andrew Potter. He was a large boy for his age, very dark of mien, with haunting eyes and a shock of touselled black hair. His eyes brooded upon me with a kind of different quality which at first challenged me but ultimately left me strangely uneasy. He was in the fifth grade, and it did not take me long to discover that he could very easily advance into the seventh or eighth, but made no effort to do so. He seemed to have only a casual tolerance for his schoolmates, and for their part, they respected him, but not out of affection so much as what struck me soon as fear. Very soon thereafter, I began to understand that this strange lad held for me the same kind of amused tolerance that he held for his schoolmates.

Perhaps it was inevitable that the challenge of this pupil should lead me to watch him as surreptitiously as I could, and as the circumstances of teaching a one-room school permitted. As a result, I became aware of a vaguely disquieting fact; from time to time, Andrew Potter responded to some stimulus beyond the apprehension of my senses, reacting precisely as if someone had called to him, sitting up, growing alert, and wearing the air of someone listening to sounds beyond my own hearing, in the same attitude assumed by animals hearing sounds beyond the pitch-levels of the human ear.

My curiosity quickened by this time, I took the first opportunity to ask about him. One of the eighth-grade boys, Wilbur Dunlock, was in the habit on occasion of staying after school and helping with the cursory cleaning that the room needed.

'Wilbur,' I said to him late one afternoon. 'I notice you don't seem to pay much attention to Andrew Potter, none of you. Why?'

He looked at me, a lttle distrustfully, and pondered his answer before he shrugged and replied, 'He's not like us.'

'In what way?'

He shook his head. 'He don't care if we let him play with us or not. He don't want to.'

He seemed reluctant to talk, but by dint of repeated questions I drew from him certain spare information. The Potters lived deep in the hills to the west along an all but abandoned branch of the main road that led through the hills. Their farm stood in a little valley locally known as Witches' Hollow which Wilbur described as 'a bad place.' There were only four of them — Andrew, an older sister, and their parents. They did not 'mix' with other people of the district, not even with the Dunlocks, who were their nearest neighbours, living but half a mile from the school itself, and thus, perhaps, four miles from Witches' Hollow, with woods separating the two farms.

More than this he could not—or would not—say.

About a week later, I asked Andrew Potter to remain after school. He offered no objection, appearing to take my request as a matter of course. As soon as the other children had gone, he came up to my desk and stood there waiting, his dark eyes fixed expectantly on me, and just the shadow of a smile on his full lips.

'I've been studying your grades, Andrew,' I said, 'and it seems to me that with only a little effort you could skip into the sixth—perhaps even the seventh—grade. Wouldn't you like to make that effort?'

He shrugged.

'What do you intend to do when you get out of school?'

He shrugged again.

'Are you going to high school in Arkham?'

He considered me with eyes that seemed suddenly piercing in their keenness, all lethargy gone. 'Mr Williams, I'm here because there's a law says I have to be,' he answered. 'There's no law says I have to go to high school.'

'But aren't you interested?' I pressed him.

'What I'm interested in doesn't matter. It's what my folks want that counts.'

'Well, I'm going to talk to them.' I decided on the moment. 'Come along. I'll take you home.'

For a moment something like alarm sprang into his expression, but in seconds it diminished and gave way to that air of watchful lethargy so typical of him. He shrugged and stood waiting while I slipped my books and papers into the schoolbag I habitually carried. Then he walked docilely to the car with me and got in, looking at me with a smile that could only be described as superior.

We rode through the woods in silence, which suited the mood that came upon me as soon as we had entered the hills, for the trees pressed close upon the road, and the deeper we went, the darker grew the wood, perhaps as much because of the lateness of that October day as because of the thickening of the trees. From relatively open glades, we plunged into an ancient wood, and when at last we turned down the side road—little more than a lane—to which Andrew silently pointed, I found that I was driving through a growth of very old and strangely deformed trees. I had to proceed with caution; the road was so little used that underbrush crowded upon it from both sides, and, oddly, I recognized little of it, for all my studies in botany, though once I thought I saw saxifrage, curiously mutated. I drove abruptly, without warning, into the yard before the Potter house.

The sun was now lost behind the wall of trees, and the house stood on a kind of twilight. Beyond it stretched a few fields, strung out up the valley; in one, there were cornshocks, in another stubble, in yet another pumpkins. The house itself was forbidding, low to the ground, with half a second storey, gambrel-roofed, with shuttered windows, and the outbuildings stood gaunt and stark, looking as if they had never been used. The entire farm looked deserted; the only sign of life was in a few chickens that scratched at the earth behind the house.

Had it not been that the lane along which we had travelled ended here, I would have doubted that we had reached the Potter house. Andrew flashed a glance at me, as if he sought some expression on my face to convey to him what I thought. Then he jumped lightly from the car, leaving me to follow.

He went into the house ahead of me. I heard him announce me.

· 'Brought the teacher. Mr. Williams.'

There was no answer.

Then abruptly I was in the room, lit only by an old-fashioned kerosene lamp, and there were the other three Potters—the father, a tall, stoop-shouldered man, grizzled and greying, who could not have been more than forty but looked much, much older, not so much physically as psychically—the mother, an almost obscenely fat woman—and the girl, slender, tall, and with that same air of watchful waiting that I had noticed in Andrew.

Andrew made the brief introductions, and the four of them stood or sat, waiting upon what I had to say, and somewhat uncomfortably suggesting in their attitudes that I say it and get out.

'I wanted to talk to you about Andrew,' I said. 'He shows great promise, and he could be moved up a grade or two if he'd study a little more.'

My words were not welcomed.

'I believe he's smart enough for eighth grade,' I went on, and stopped.

'If he 'uz in eighth grade,' said his father, 'he's be havin' to go to high school 'fore he 'uz old enough to git outa goin' to school. That's the law. They told me.'

I could not help thinking of what Wilbur Dunlock had told me of the reclusiveness of the Potters, and as I listened to the elder Potter, and thought of what I had heard, I was suddenly aware of a kind of tension among them, and a subtle alteration in their attitude. The moment the father stopped talking, there was a singular harmony of attitude—all four of them seemed to be listening to some inner voice, and I doubt that they heard my protest at all.

'You can't expect a boy as smart as Andrew just to come back here,' I said.

'Here's good enough,' said old Potter. 'Besides, he's ours. And don't ye go talkin' 'bout us now, Mr. Williams.'

He spoke with so latently menacing an undercurrent in his

voice that I was taken aback. At the same time I was increasingly aware of a miasma of hostility, not proceeding so much from any one or all four of them, as from the house and its setting themselves.

'Thank you,' I said. 'I'll be going.'

I turned and went out, Andrew at my heels.

Outside, Andrew said softly, 'You shouldn't be talking about us, Mr. Williams. Pa gets mad when he finds out. You talked to Wilbur Dunlock.'

I was arrested at getting into the car. With one foot on the running board, I turned. 'Did he say so?' I asked.

He shook his head. 'You did, Mr. Williams,' he said, and backed away. 'It's not what he thinks, but what he might do.'

Before I could speak again, he had darted into the house.

For a moment I stood undecided. But my decision was made for me. Suddenly, in the twilight, the house seemed to burgeon with menace, and all the surrounding woods seemed to stand waiting but to bend upon me. Indeed, I was aware of a rustling, like the whispering of wind, in all the wood, though no wind stirred, and from the house itself came a malevolence like the blow of a fist. I got into the car and drove away, with that impression of malignance at my back like the hot breath of a ravaging pursuer.

I reached my room in Arkham at last, badly shaken. Seen in retrospect, I had undergone an unsettling psychic experience; there was no other explanation for it. I had the unavoidable conviction that, however blindly, I had thrust myself in far deeper waters than I knew, and the very unexpectedness of the experience made it the more chilling. I could not eat for the wonder of what went on in that house in Witches' Hollow, of what it was that bound the family together, chaining them to that place, preventing a promising lad like Andrew Potter even from the most fleeting wish to leave that dark valley and go out into a brighter world.

I lay for most of that night, sleepless, filled with a nameless dread for which all explanation eluded me, and when I slept at last my sleep was filled with hideously disturbing dreams, in which beings far beyond my mundane imagination held the stage, and cataclysmic events of the utmost terror and horror took place. And when I rose next morning, I felt that somehow I had touched upon a world totally alien to my kind.

I reached the school early that morning. But Wilbur Dunlock was there before me. His eyes met mine with sad reproach. I could not imagine what had happened to disturb this usually friendly pupil.

'You shouldn't a told Andrew Potter we talked about him,' he said with a kind of unhappy resignation.

'I didn't, Wilbur.'

'I know I didn't. So you must have,' he said. And then, 'Six of our cows got killed last night, and the shed where they were was crushed down on 'em.'

I was momentarily too startled to reply. 'A sudden windstorm,' I began, but he cut me off.

'Weren't no wind last night, Mr. Williams. And the cows were smashed.'

'You surely cannot think that the Potters had anything to do with this, Wilbur,' I cried.

He gave me a weary look—the look of one who *knows*, meeting the glance of one who should know but cannot understand, and said nothing more.

This was even more upsetting than my experience of the previous evening. He at least was convinced that there was a connection between our conversation about the Potter family and the Dunlocks' loss of half a dozen cows. And he was convinced with so deep a conviction that I knew without trying that nothing I could say would shake it.

When Andrew Potter came in, I looked in vain for any sign that anything out of the ordinary had taken place since last I had seen him.

Somehow I got through that day. Immediately after the close of the school session, I hastened into Arkham and went to the office of the *Arkham Gazette*, the editor of which had been kind enough, as a member of the local District Board of Education, to find my room for me. He was an elderly man, almost seventy, and might presumably know what I wanted to find out.

My appearance must have conveyed something of my agitation, for when I walked into his office, his eyebrows lifted, and he said, 'What's got your dander up, Mr. Williams?'

I made some attempt to dissemble, since I could put my hand upon nothing tangible, and, viewed in the cold light of day, what I might have said would have sounded almost hysterical to an impartial listener. I said only, 'I'd like to know something about a Potter family that lives in Witches' Hollow, west of the school.'

He gave me an enigmatic glance. 'Never heard of old Wizard Potter?' he asked. And, before I could answer, he went on, 'No, of course, you're from Brattleboro. We could hardly expect Vermonters to know about what goes on in the Massachusetts back country. He lived there first. An old man when I first knew him. And these Potters were distant relatives, lived in Upper Michigan, inherited the property and came to live there when Wizard Potter died.'

'But what do you know about them?' I persisted.

'Nothing but what everybody else knows,' he said. 'When they came, they were nice friendly people. Now they talk to nobody, seldom come out—and there's all that talk about missing animals from the farms in the district. The people tie that all up.'

Thus begun, I questioned him at length.

I listened to a bewildering enigma of half-told tales, hints, legends and lore utterly beyond my comprehension. What seemed to be incontrovertible was a distant cousinship between Wizard Potter and one Wizard Whateley of nearby Dunwich—'a bad lot,' the editor called him; the solitary way of life of old Wizard Potter, and the incredible length of time he had lived; the fact that people generally shunned Witches' Hollow. What seemed to be sheer fantasy was the superstitious lore—that Wizard Potter had 'called something down from the sky, and it lived with him or in him until he died';—that a late traveller, found in a dying state along the main road, had gasped out something about 'that thing with the feelers—slimy, rubbery thing with the suckers on its feelers' that came out of the woods and attacked him—and a good deal more of the same kind of lore.

When he finished, the editor scribbled a note to the librarian at Miskatonic University in Arkham, and handed it to me. 'Tell him to let you look at that book. You may learn something.' He shrugged. 'And you may not. Young people now-days take the world with a lot of salt.'

I went supperless to pursue my search for the special knowledge I felt I needed, if I were to save Andrew Potter for a better life. For it was this rather than the satisfaction of my curiosity that impelled me. I made my way to the library of Miskatonic University, looked up the librarian, and handed him the editor's note.

The old man gave me a sharp look, said, 'Wait here, Mr. Williams,' and went off with a ring of keys. So the book, whatever it was, was kept under lock and key.

I waited for what seemed an interminable time. I was now beginning to feel some hunger, and to question my unseemly haste—and yet I felt that there was little time to be lost, though I could not define the catastrophe I hoped to avert. Finally the librarian came, bearing an ancient tome, and brought it around to a table within his range of vision. The book's title was in Latin—*Necronomicon*—though its author was evidently an Arabian, *Abdul Alhazred*, and its text was in somewhat archaic English.

I began to read with interest which soon turned to complete bewilderment. The book evidently concerned ancient, alien races, invaders of earth, great mythical beings called Ancient Ones and Elder Gods, with outlandish names like Cthulhu and Hastur, Shub-Niggurath and Azathoth, Dagon and Ithaqua and Wendigo and Cthugha, all involved in some kind of plan to dominate earth and served by some of its peoples—the Tcho-Tcho, and the Deep Ones, and the like. It was a book filled with cabbalistic lore, incantations, and what purported to be an account of a great interplanetary battle between the Elder Gods and the Ancient Ones and of the survival of cults and servitors in isolated and remote places on our planet as well as on sister planets. What this rigmarole had to do with my immediate problem, with the ingrown and strange Potter family and their longing for solitude and their anti-social way of life, was completely beyond me.

How long I would have gone on reading, I do not know. I was interrupted presently by the awareness of being studied by a stranger, who stood not far from me with his eyes moving from the book I was busy reading to me. Having caught my eye, he made so bold as to come over to my side.

'Forgive me,' he said, 'But what in this book interests a country school teacher?'

'I wonder now myself,' I said.

He introduced himself as Professor Martin Keane. 'I may say, sir,' he added, 'that I know this book practically by heart.'

'A farrago of superstitution.'

'Do you think so?'

'Emphatically.'

'You have lost the quality of wonder, Mr. Williams. Tell me, if you will, what brought you to this book—'

I hesitated, but Professor Keane's personality was persuasive and inspired confidence.

'Let us walk, if you don't mind,' I said.

He nodded.

I returned the book to the librarian, and joined my new-found friend. Haltingly, as clearly as I could, I told him about Andrew Potter, the house in Witches' Hollow, my strange psychic experience—even the curious coincidence of Dunlock's cows. To all this he listened without interruption, indeed, with a singular absorption. I explained at last that my motive in looking into the background of Witches' Hollow was solely to do something for my pupil.

'A little research,' he said, 'would have informed you that many strange events have taken place in such remote places as Dunwich and Innsmouth—even Arkham and Witches' Hollow,' he said when I finished. 'Look around you at these ancient houses with their shuttered rooms and ill-lit fanlights. How many strange events have taken place under those gambrel roofs! We shall never know. But let us put aside the question of belief! One may not need to see the embodiment of evil to believe in it, Mr. Williams. I should like to be of some small service to the boy in this matter. May I?'

'By all means!'

'It may be perilous—to you as well as to him.'

'I am not concerned about myself.'

'But I assure you, it cannot be any more perilous to the boy than his present position. Even death for him is less perilous.'

'You speak in riddles, Professor.'

'Let it be better so, Mr. Williams. But come—we are at my residence. Pray come in.'

We went into one of those ancient houses of which Professor Keane had spoken. I walked into the musty past, for the rooms were filled with books and all manner of antiquities. My host took me into what was evidently his sitting-room, swept a chair clear of books, and invited me to wait while he busied himself on the second floor.

He was not, however, gone very long—not even long enough for me to assimilate the curious atmosphere of the room in which I waited. When he came back he carried what I saw at once were objects of stone, roughly in the shape of five-pointed stars. He put five of them into my hands.

'Tomorrow after school — if the Potter boy is there — you must contrive to touch him with one of these, and keep it fixed upon him,' said my host. 'There are two other conditions. You must keep one of these at least on your person at all times, and you must keep all thought of the stone and what you are about to do out of your mind. These beings have a telepathic sense—an ability to read your thoughts.'

Startled, I recalled Andrew's charging me with having talked about them with Wilbur Dunlock.

'Should I not know what these are?' I asked.

'If you can abate your doubts for the time being,' my host answered with a grim smile. 'These stones are among the thousands bearing the Seal of R'lyeh which closed the prisons of the Ancient Ones. They are the seals of the Elder Gods.'

'Professor Keane, the age of superstition is past,' I protested.

'Mr. Williams — the wonder of life and its mysteries is never past,' he retorted. 'If the stone has no meaning, it has no power. If it has no power, it cannot affect young Potter. And it cannot protect you.'

'From what?'

'From the power behind the malignance you felt at the house in Witches' Hollow,' he answered. 'Or was this too superstition?' He smiled. 'You need not answer. I know your answer. If something happens when you put the stone upon the boy, he cannot be allowed to go back home. You must bring him here to me. Are you agreed?'

'Agreed,' I answered.

That next day was interminable, not only because of the imminence of crisis, but because it was extremely difficult to keep my mind blank before the inquiring gaze of Andrew Potter. Moreover, I was conscious as never before of the wall of pulsing malignance at my back, emanating from the wild country there, a tangible menace hidden in a pocket of the dark hills. But the hours passed, however slowly, and just before dismissal I asked Andrew Potter to wait after the others had gone.

And again he assented with that casual air tantamount almost to insolence, so that I was compelled to ask myself whether he were worth 'saving' as I thought of saving him in the depths of my mind.

But I persevered. I had hidden the stone in my car, and, once the others were gone, I asked Andrew to step outside with me.

At this point I felt both helpless and absurd. I, a college graduate, about to attempt what for me seemed inevitably the kind of mumbo-jumbo that belonged to the African wilderness. And for a few moments, as I walked stiffly from the school house toward the car I almost flagged, almost simply invited Andrew to get into the car to be driven home.

But I did not. I reached the car with Andrew at my heels, reached in, seized a stone to slip into my own pocket, seized another, and turned with lightning rapidity to press the stone to Andrew's forehead.

Whatever I expected to happen, it was not what took place.

For, at the touch of the stone, an expression of the utmost horror shone in Andrew Potter's eyes; in a trice, his gave way to poignant anguish; a great cry of terror burst from his lips. He flung his arms wide, scattering his books, wheeled as far as he could with my hold upon him, shuddered, and would have fallen, had I not caught him and lowered him, foaming at the mouth, to the ground. And then I was conscious of a great, cold wind which whirled about us and was gone, bending the grasses and the flowers, rippling the edge of the wood, and tearing away the leaves at the outer band of trees.

Driven by my own terror, I lifted Andrew Potter into the car, laid the stone on his chest, and drove as fast as I could into Arkham, seven miles away. Professor Keane was waiting, no whit surprised at my coming. And he had expected that I would bring Andrew Potter, for he had made a bed ready for him, and together we put him into it, after which Keane administered a sedative.

Then he turned to me. 'Now then, there's no time to be lost. They'll come to look for him—the girl probably first. We must get back to the school house at once.'

But now the full meaning and horror of what had happened to Andrew Potter had dawned upon me, and I was so shaken that it was necessary for Keane to push me from the room and half drag me out of the house. And again, as I set down these words so long after the terrible events of that night, I find myself trembling with that apprehension and fear which seize hold of a man who comes for the first time face to face with the vast unknown and knows how puny and meaningless he is against that cosmic immensity. I knew in that moment that what I had read in that forbidden book at the Miskatonic Library was not a farrago of superstition, but the key to a hitherto unsuspected revelation perhaps far, far older than mankind in the universe. I did not dare to think of what Wizard Potter had called down from the sky.

I hardly heard Professor Keane's words as he urged me to discard my emotional reaction and think of what had happened in scientific, more clinical fashion. After all, I had now accomplished my objective—Andrew Potter was saved. But to insure it, he must be made free of the others, who would surely follow him and find him. I thought only of what waiting horror that quartet of country people from Michigan had walked into when they came to take up possession of the solitary farm in Witches' Hollow.

I drove blindly back to the school. There, at Professor Keane's behest, I put on the lights and sat with the door open to the warm night, while he concealed himself behind the building to wait upon their coming. I had to steel myself in order to blank out my mind and take up that vigil.

On the edge of night, the girl came . . .

And after she had undergone the same experience as her brother, and lay beside the desk, the star-shaped stone on her breast, their father showed up in the doorway. All was darkness now, and he carried a gun. He had no need to ask what had happened; he *knew*. He stood wordless, pointed to his daughter and the stone on her breast, and raised his gun. His inference was plain—if I did not remove the stone, he meant to shoot. Evidently this was the contingency the professor expected, for he came upon Potter from the rear and touched him with the stone.

Afterwards we waited for two hours—in vain, for Mrs. Potter.

'She isn't coming,' said Professor Keane at last. 'She harbours the seat of its intelligence—I had thought it would be the man. Very well—we have no choice—we must go to Witches' Hollow. These two can be left here.'

We drove through the darkness, making no attempt at secrecy, for the professor said the 'thing' in the house in the Hollow 'knew' we were coming but could not reach us past the talisman of the stone. We went through that close pressing forest, down the narrow lane where the queer undergrowth seemed to reach out toward us in the glow of the head lights, into the Potter yard.

The house stood dark save for a wan glow of lamplight in one room.

Professor Keane leaped from the car with his little bag of star-shaped stones, and went around sealing the house—with a stone at each of the two doors, and one at each of the windows, through one of which we could see the woman sitting at the kitchen table—stolid, watchful, *aware*, no longer dissembling, looking unlike that tittering woman I had seen in this house not long ago, but rather like some great sentient beast at bay.

When he had finished, my companion went around to the front and, by means of brush collected from the yard and piled against the door, set fire to the house heedless of my protests.

Then he went back to the window to watch the woman, explaining that only fire could destroy the elemental force, but that he hoped, still, to save Mrs. Potter. 'Perhaps you'd better not watch, Williams.'

I did not heed him. Would that I had—and so spared myself the dreams that invade my sleep even yet! I stood at the window behind him and watched what went on in that room—for the smell of smoke was now permeating the house. Mrs. Potter—or what animated her gross body—started up, went awkwardly to the back door, retreated, to the window, retreated from it, and came back to the centre of the room, between the table and the wood stove, not yet fired against the coming cold. There she fell to the floor, heaving and writhing.

The room filled slowly with smoke, hazing about the yellow lamp, making the room indistinct—but not indistinct enough to conceal completely what went on in the course of that terrible struggle on the floor, where Mrs. Potter threshed about as if in mortal convulsion and slowly, half visibly, something or other

69

took shape—an incredible amorphous mass, only half glimpsed in the smoke, tentacled, shimmering, with a cold intelligence and a physical coldness that I could feel through the window. The thing rose like a cloud above the now motionless body of Mrs. Potter, and then fell upon the stove and drained into it like vapour!

'The stove!' cried Professor Keane, and fell back.

Above us, out of the chimney, came a spreading blackness, like smoke, gathering itself briefly there. Then it hurtled like a lightning bolt aloft, into the stars, in the direction of the Hyades, back to that place from which old Wizard Potter had called it into himself, away from where it had lain in wait for the Potters to come from Upper Michigan and afford it new host on the face of earth.

We managed to get Mrs. Potter out of the house, much shrunken now, but alive.

On the remainder of that night's events there is no need to to dwell—how the professor waited until fire had consumed the house to collect his store of star-shaped stones, of the reuniting of the Potter family—freed from the curse of Witches' Hollow and determined never to return to that haunted valley—of Andrew, who, when we came to waken him, was talking in his sleep of 'great winds that fought and tore' and a 'place by the Lake of Hali where they live in glory forever.'

What it was that old Wizard Potter had called down from the stars, I lacked the courage to ask, but I knew that it touched upon secrets better left unknown to the races of men, secrets I would never have become aware of had I not chanced to take District School Number Seven, and had among my pupils the strange boy who was Andrew Potter.

Is the Devil a Gentleman?

SEABURY QUINN

It had been a day of strange weather, a day the calendar declared to be late April and the thermometer proclaimed to be March or November. From dawn till early dark the rain had spattered down, chill, persistent, deceptive, making it feel many degrees colder than it really was, but just at sunset it had cleared and a sort of angry yellow half-light had spilled from a sky of streaky black against a bank of blood-red clouds. Now, while the dying wind was groping with chill-stiffened fingers at the window-casings, a fire blazed on the study hearth, its comforting rose glow a gleaming island in the gathering shadows, its reflection daubing ever-changing pattern on the walls and tightly-drawn curtains.

'On such a night,' the Bishop quoted inexactly as he helped himself to brandy, 'mine enemy's dog, though he had bit me, I would not turn away from my door.'

Dr. Bentley, rector of St. Chrysostom's, dropped a second lump of sugar in his coffee and said nothing. He knew the Bishop, and had known him since their student days. When he quoted Shakespeare he was really searching through the lumber rooms of memory for a story, and there were few who had a better store of anecdotes than the Right Reverend Richard Chauncev, missionary, soldier, preacher and ecclesiastical executive, worldly man of God and godly man of the world. He'd looked forward to Dick's coming down for confirmation, and had made a point of asking Kitteringson in to dinner. Kitteringson was all right, of course; good, earnest worker, a good preacher and a good churchman, but a trifle too—how should he put it?—too dogmatic. If you couldn't find it in the writings of the Fathers of the Church or the Thirty-nine Articles he was against a proposition, whatever it might be. A session with the Bishop would be good for him.

'Good stuff in the lad,' thought Dr. Bentley as he studied his junior covetly. A rather strong, intelligent face he had, but marked by asceticism, the face of one who might be either an unyielding martyr or a merciless inquisitor. Now he was leaning forward almost eagerly, and the firelight did things to his earnest face—made it look like one of those old medieval monks in the old masters' paintings.

'I've been wondering all day, sir,' he told Bishop Chauncey, 'what you meant when you told the confirmation class they should use common sense about religious prejudices. Surely, there may be no compromise with evil—'

'I shouldn't care to lay that down as a precept,' the Bishop answered with a low chuckle. 'We're told the Devil can quote Scripture for his purposes; why shouldn't Christians make use of the powers of darkness in a proper case?'

Young Dr. Kitteringson was aghast. 'Make use of Satan?' he faltered. 'Have dealings with the arch-fiend—'

'Precisely, son. Shakespeare might have been more truthful than poetical when he declared the Prince of Darkness is a gentleman.'

'I can't conceive of such a thing!' the younger man retorted. 'All our experiences tell us—'

'All?' cut in Bishop Chauncey softly, and the young rector fell hesitant before the level irony of his gaze. 'How old are you, son?'

'Thirty-two, sir, but I've read the writings of the Fathers of the Early Church, and one and all they tell us that to compromise with evil is a sin against—' He stopped, a little abashed at the look of tolerant amusement on his senior's face, then: 'Can you name even one case when compromise with evil didn't end disastrously for all concerned, sir?' he challenged.

'Yes, I think I can,' the Bishop passed the brandy sniffer back and forth beneath his nostrils, inhaled the bouquet of the old cognac appreciatively, then took a delicate, approving sip. 'I think I can, son. Like you, I have to call upon my reading to sustain me, but unlike you I can't claim ecclesiastical authority for my writers. One of them, indeed, was an ancestor of mine, a great-grandfather several times removed.'

The gloom that waited just beyond the moving edge of firelight seemed flowing forward, like a slowly rising, stagnant tide, and a blazing ember falling to the layer of sand beneath the burning logs sent a sudden shaft of light across the intervening shade, casting a quick shadow of the Bishop on the farther wall. An odd shadow it was, not like the rubicund, grey-haired churchman, but queerly elongated and distorted, so that it appeared to be the shade of a lean man with gaunt and predatory features, muffled in a cloak and leaning forward at the shoulders, like one intent—almost in the act of pouncing.

Kundre Maltby (said the Bishop, drawing thoughtfully at his cigar so its recurrent glow etched his face in alternate red highlight and black shadow) was a confessed witch, and witches, as you know, are those who have made solemn compact with the Evil One.

She was a Swedish girl—at least she claimed that she was Swedish—whom Captain Pelatiah Maltby had found somewhere in his travels, married, and brought back to Danby by Salem. Who she really was nobody knew.

Captain Maltby's ship, the *Bountiful Adventure,* came on her Easter Monday morning, clinging to a hatch-grating some twenty miles or so off the Madeira coast. He'd cleared from Funchal the night before, swearing that he'd never make the port again, for the Portuguese had celebrated Easter with an *auto da fé* at which a hundred condemned witches had been burned, and the sight of the poor wretches' sufferings sickened him. When he asked the castaway her name she told him it was Kundre, and said her ship had been the *Blenkinge* of Stockholm, wrecked three days before.

Maltby marvelled at this information, for he had been in the Madeiras for a whole week, and there had been no storm, not even a light squall. But there the girl was, lashed to the floating hatch-top, virtually nude and all but dead with thirst and starvation. Moreover, she had very winning ways and more than a fair share of beauty, so Captain Maltby asked no further questions, but put in at New York and married her before he brought the *Bountiful Adventure* up the coast to Danby.

Their life together seems to have been ideal, possibly idyllic. He was a raw-boned, tough-thewed son of New England, hard as flint outside and practical as the multiplication tables within. But it was from such ancestry that Whittier and Holmes and Bryant and Longfellow sprang, and probably beneath his workaday exterior Pelatiah Maltby had a poet's soul. They had twin children, a boy and a girl. At Pelatiah's insistence the girl was named for her mother, but Kundre chose the name of Micah for the boy, for in the whole Scripture she liked best that Prophet's question, 'What doth the Lord require of thee, but to do justly, and to love mercy, and to walk humbly with thy God?'

She took to transplantation like a hardy flower, and grew and flourished on New England soil. From all accounts she must have been a beauty in a heavy Nordic way, a true woman of the sea. Full six feet tall she was, and strong as any man, yet with all the gracious curves of womanhood. Her hair, they say, was golden. Not merely yellow, but that metallic shade of gold which, catching glints of outside light, seems to hold a light of its own. And her skin was white as sea-foam, and her eyes the bright blue-green of the ice of the fjords, and her lips were red as sunset on the ocean when a storm has blown itself away.

Prosperity came with her, too. The winds were always favourable to Captain Maltby's ship. He made the longest voyages in the shortest time. When other ships were set upon by tempests and battered till they were mere hulks he came safely through the raving storms or missed them altogether, and his enterprises always prospered. Foreign traders sold him goods at laughably low prices, or bought the cargoes that he brought at prices that astonished him.

He brought back treasures from the far corners of the earth, silks from Cathay and Nippon, carved coral from the South Sea Isles, pearls from Java, diamonds from Africa, a comb of solid beaten gold from India—and the golden comb seemed pallid when she drew it through the golden spate of her loosed golden hair.

The neighbours were first amazed, then wondering, finally suspicious. Experience had taught them Providence dealt even-handedly with men and balanced its smiles with its frowns. Yet Pelatiah Maltby always won. He never had to drain a cup of vinegar to compensate him for the many heady cups of the wine of success he quaffed.

It was Captain Joel Newton who brought matters to a head. He and Captain Maltby had been rivals many years. His pew was just across the aisle from Maltby's in the meeting house, his wife sat where she could not help but see the worldly gewgaws Maltby lavished on Kundre, and Abigail Newton's tongue had an edge like that of a new-filed adze, and her jealousy the bitter bite of acid. Joel Newton heard himself compared to Pelatiah Maltby, with small advantage, every Lord's Day after service, and, driven by the lash of a shrew's tongue, he determined to find the key to Maltby's constant success, and set himself deliberately to trail the *Bountiful Adventure* from one port to another.

Not that it helped him. The *Bountiful Adventure* outsailed him every trip, and when he came into a foreign berth he found that Maltby had been there before him, secured what trade there was, and sailed away.

They came face to face at last at Tamatave in Madagascar. Maltby had traded rum and salted fish and tobacco for a holdful of rich native silver, and the local traders had no thought of laying in new stocks for months. Newton's ship was loaded to capacity with just the wares that Maltby had disposed of so profitably, there was no market for his cargo, his food was running low, and ruin stared him in the face.

Both had taken more of the French wines the inn purveyed than was their custom. Maltby was flushed with success, Newton bitter with the mordancy of disappointment. 'Had I a witch-woman for wife I'd always fare well, too,' he told his rival.

'How quotha?' Maltby asked. 'What meanest, knave? My Kundre is the fairest, sweetest bloom—'

'As ever sank its taproots deep in hell,' his rival finished for him, 'Oh, don't 'ee think to fool us, Neighbour Maltby! We know what 'tis that always sends the fair winds at thy tail when others lie becalmed. We know what 'tis that makes the heathen take thy wares at such great prices, and pay thee ten times what thou'd hoped to get. Aye, and we know whence comes thy witch-mate, too—how the Papishers had burned a drove of warlocks in the Madeiras the day before ye found her floating in the ocean. She said her vessel had been wrecked three days before, but had there been a storm? Thou knowest well there had not. Did'st offer her free passage back to the island, and did she take thy offer kindly?'

Now this was a poser, for Pelatiah had offered to set Kundre on shore at Funchal when he rescued her, and she had refused tearfully, and begged him to hold to his course.

'And why?' asked Captain Newton as he warmed to his task of denunciation. 'I'll tell 'ee why, my fine bucko—because she was a cursed witch who'd slipped between the Papists' fingers and made use of thee to ferry her to safety. Thinkest thou she loves thee? Faugh! While thou'rt away she wantons it with every man 'twixt Danby and old Salem Town——'

'Thou liar!' The scandalous words were like to have been Joel's last, for Pelatiah drew his hanger and made for him with intent to stab the slander down his throat with cold steel, but Joel was just a thought too quick.

Before his rival reached him he jerked a pistol from his waistband and let fly, striking Captain Maltby fairly in the chest. Afterwards he boasted that it was a silver bullet he had used, since, as everybody knew, witches, warlocks and were-beasts were impervious to lead, but vulnerable to silver missiles.

However that might be Captain Maltby halted in mid-stride, and his hanger fell with a clatter from his unnerved hand. He hiccoughed once and tried to draw a breath that stopped before he had it in, sagged at the knees, fell on his side and died. But with that last unfinished breath they say he whispered, 'Kundre dearest, they have done for me and will for thee if so be that they can. God have thee in His keeping—'

Maltby, of course, was a Protestant, and the only Christian cemetery in the town was Catholic. It was not possible a heretic should lie in consecrated ground, but the missionary priest took counsel with the rabbi of the little Jewish congregation and arranged to buy a grave-site in the Hebrew burying ground.

There was no ordained minister of his faith to do the final service for Maltby, so the priest and rabbi stood beside his grave, and one said Christian prayers in Latin, and the other Jewish prayers in Hebrew, while the grim-faced sailors from New England stood by and marvelled at this show of charity in those they had been taught to hate, and responded with tear-choked 'A-mens' when prayers were done and time had come to heap the earth upon the body sewn in sailcloth in lieu of a coffin.

It was a Wednesday in mid-April when the killing took place, and Kundre, so the story goes, was sitting beside the brooklet that ran through her back-lot. The weather was unseasonably warm, and her children waded in the stream and searched for buds of ground-rose while she sunned and bleached the hair that was her greatest pride—or vanity, according to the neighbours' wives. Suddenly she raised her head like one who listens to a hail from far away, shook back her clouding hair and cupped one hand to her ear to sit there statue-still for a long moment. Then, with a cry that seemed to be the echo of her riven heart-strings' breaking, she called out, 'Pelatiah! Oh beloved!' and fell forward on her face beside the brooklet, lying with her arms outstretched before her like a diver's when he strikes the water, while her great, heroically-formed body twitched and jerked, and little, dreadful moans came bubbling from her lips, like blood that wells and bubbles from a mortal wound.

Presently she rose and dried her eyes and went into the house where she laid away her gown of crisp blue linen and put on widow's weeds before she sought Ezekiel Martin the stone-mason and ordered him to cut and set a gravestone in the village church-yard. You could see that tombstone now if you should go to Danby burying ground. It reads:

Sacred to the memory of
PELATIAH MALTBY
Chriftian man & feacaptain
Moft foully done to death by jealoufie
at Tamatave in Madagafcie

Now, you'll allow it would be cause for comment, even in these days when extrasensory perceptions are taken as more or less established facts, for a woman to become aware of her husband's death half-way round the world from her at the very moment of its happening. The circumstances caused comment in mid-seventeenth century New England, too, but not at all of the same kind. Everybody dreaded sorcery and witchcraft then, and in every unexplained occurrence men saw Satan's ungloved hand. So when Kundre went forth in her mourning clothes, sorrowing dry-eyed at the empty grave where she had placed the tombstone, neighbours looked at her from beneath lowered lids, and when she went to divine service at the meeting house the tithing man went past her hurriedly, and hardly paused to hold the alms basin before her, though he knew it would be heavier by a gold piece minted with the symbol of King Charles' majesty when he withdrew it.

In August came the *Bountiful Adventure* with her ensign flying at half-mast, and Captain Maltby's death was confirmed by the sorrowing seamen.

But what became of Captain Joel Newton and his ship the *Crystal Wave* nobody ever knew. He had set sail from Tamatava the same day he shot Maltby, for everyone agreed he had provoked the quarrel, and the commandant of the garrison threatened his arrest unless he drew his anchor from the harbour-mud at once. The rest was silence. Neither stick nor spar nor broken bit of wreckage ever washed ashore to show the *Crystal Wave's* fate, or that of Captain Joel Newton and the twenty seamen of his crew.

Voyages of a year or even two years were the rule those days, and it was not until King Charles had been beheaded and the Lord Protector proclaimed that Abigail Newton descended from the 'widow's watch' that topped her square-roofed house beside the harbour and changed her home-spun gown of blue for one of black linsey woolsey, then sent for Zeke Martin the mason to cut and set a stone in Danby churchyard.

The twenty widows of the *Crystal Wave's* crew also went in mourning, and bewailed their joint and several losses piteously. When they passed Kundre in the street they looked away, but when she'd gotten safely past they spit upon the ground and muttered 'witch!' and 'Devil's-hag!'

Kundre was a Swedish woman, and though the good folk of Danby had small use for King James's politics and even less for his religion, they were with him to a man in his views on witchcraft. Moreover, they recalled how Scandinavian witches had raised storms and tempests to prevent the Princess Anne from reaching Scotland where her marriage to King James was to be solemnized, and some of the more learned in the village knew the legends of *Sangreal* and remembered that the temptress who all but kept the Holy Grail from Parsifal was named Kundry. There seemed little difference between her name and Kundre's. Kundry of the legend was a witch damned past redemption, might not Kundre—the strange outland woman who knew of her husband's death four months before the news came home—also be a potent witch?

It seemed entirely possible and even probable, and when the widowed Abigail met widowed Kundre in the village street and taxed her with destroying both the *Crystal Wave's* master and crew by witchcraft, something happened to confirm the worst suspicions.

'Thou art a wicked, Devil-vowed and wanton witch!' said Abigail in hearing of at least three neighbour women. 'By thy vile arts thou raised a monstrous storm and sank the *Crystal Wave* and all her people in the ocean.'

Kundre looked at her, and in her ice-blue eyes there seemed to kindle a slow light like that which the aurora borealis makes on winter nights. 'Thy tongue is dipped in venom like a serpent's, Goody Newton,' she replied in the deep voice which was her Nordic heritage. 'It never wags except to hurt thy neighbours, so 'twere best thou never used it hereafter.'

Whether from the look in Kundre's eyes, or from astonishment that anyone should dare to tell her to keep still we do not know, but it was amply attested that Abigail for once had no reply to make, and we find in the old town records of Danby that on the evening after this encounter she lost her power of speech completely. More, she lost the use of her tongue, for it swelled and swelled until she could not keep it in her mouth, and she could take no nourishment but liquids, and those with greatest difficulty.

In the light of present-day medical knowledge it would not be too difficult to attribute her misfortune to that rare condition known as macroglossia or hypertrophy of the tongue, which doctors tell us is due to engorgement and dilation of the lymph channels. Most of us who have served in hospitals have seen such cases, where the swollen tongue hangs from the mouth and gives the patient a peculiarly idiotic look. But medicine was far from an exact science those days, and besides there was the testimony of the women who had seen the curse of silence laid on Abigail. Three hours after sunset Kundre was 'spoken against' as a witch and duly lodged in Danby jail.

By the common law of England torture was forbidden to force a prisoner to accuse himself, but by the witchcraft statutes of King James certain "tests" which differed from torture neither in degree nor kind were permitted. One of these was known as "swimming," for it was believed a witch's body was so buoyed up with evil that it could not sink in water.

Accordingly, upon the second day of her confinement Kundre was brought out to be "swum." Stripped to her shift they led her from the jail to the horse-pond which served the village as reservoir and ornamental lake at once, forced her to sit cross-legged on the ground and tied her right thumb to her left great toe, her right great toe to her left thumb with heavy linen thread which had been waxed for greater strength, and to make it cut more deeply in the tender flesh. Then over her they dropped a linen bedsheet, tumbled her all helpless as she was upon her side and tied the sheet's loose ends together, exactly as a modern housewife makes a laundry bundle ready. A rope was fastened to the knotted sheet and willing hands laid hold on it and dragged it out into the water.

Now here we have a choice between the natural and the supernatural. We have all seen the properties of wet cloth to retain the air and resist water. The device known as water wings with which so many children learn to swim is simply a cloth bladder wet before inflation, and as long as outside pressure is evenly applied it will support surprisingly large weights in calm water.

Perhaps it was as natural a phenomenon as this that kept the accused woman afloat on the calm surface of the village horse-pond. Perhaps, again, it was something more sinister. At any rate, the sheeted bundle bobbed and floated on the quiet surface of the pool as easily as if it had been filled with cork, and a great shout went up from the spectators 'She swims! She swims; it is the judgement of just Heaven; she is a proven witch!'

Her trial lasted a full day, and people came from miles about to hear the evidence poured on her. Ezekiel Martin the stonemason told how she came to him and ordered him to cut the tombstone for a man whose limbs were scarcely stiff in death, though none could know that he had died until his ship came a full four months later.

There was no dearth of testimony concerning the fine winds and weather that had been her husband's portion since he married her, or concerning the storms that had plagued his rivals.

Abigail Newton stood up in court that all might see her swollen tongue, and though she could not speak, she went through an elaborate dumb-show of the way the curse had been laid on her. Less reticent, Flee-from-the-Wrath-to-Come Epsworth, Rebecca Norris and Susan Clayton told under oath how they had seen and heard Kundre strike Abigail with speechlessness.

A tithe of such evidence would have been enough to hang her, and the jury took but fifteen minutes to deliberate upon their verdict, which, of course, was guilty.

Asked what she had to say in her defence before the court pronounced sentence, she made a seemly curtsey to the judge and answered without hesitation ' 'Tis true I am a witch as ye have charged me. Long years agone my sire and dam made compact with the Prince of Evil and bound me by their covenant, but never have I used my power to hurt a living creature, brute or human. That I should wish my man to prosper was but natural. Thus far I used my power over wind and tides, but no farther. Whether Heaven punished Goodman Newton for the foul murder that he did on my poor man I cannot say. I know naught of the matter, nor did I lift a finger to bring Heaven's retribution on him. "Vengeance is mine, I will repay," saith the Lord.

'As for the swollen tongue of yon shrew, belike it is the malice of her black and jealous heart that bloats it. As to that I cannot answer; but hark ye, neighbours, if I had the power to release her I'd not use it. The town is better for her silence, as I wis ye all agree.'

With that she made another curtsey to the judge and stood there silent, waiting sentence: 'Since, therefore, Goodwife Kundre Maltby hath by her own confession admitted she was justly tried and convicted, so let her on account of her bond with the Devil and on account of the witchcraft she hath practised, be hanged by the neck until she be dead.'

The usual formula in hanging cases was for the court to add, 'and may God have mercy on thy soul,' but such a sentiment seemed obviously out of place here, and the judge forbore to express it.

They carried out the sentence next day, and a mighty crowd was gathered for the spectacle. The members of the trained band were much put to it to control the rabble when the hangman drove his cart beneath the gallows tree and made the hemp fast to her neck.

She wore her widow's weeds to execution, and round her neck was clasped a slender chain of some base metal with a flat pendant like a coin hung from it. It was the only ornament she'd had when Pelatiah found her floating on the grating, and she had laid it by when they were married. Now, through a whim, perhaps, she chose to wear it at her death.

They'd let her children visit her in jail the night before, and she had sent the girl back for the bauble. 'Look well on it, my sweet,' she told the child when it was clasped about her neck. 'The time may come when thou'lt have need of it, and if it comes thou shalt not cry for it in vain.'

As the hangman bound her elbows to her sides before he slipped the noose beneath her chin she begged him, 'Leave the worthless chain in place when thy grim task is done, good Peter Grimes. In my left shoe thou'lt find a golden sovereign hidden to repay thee for thy work. Take it and welcome, but if thou take'st the chain and pendant from me—a witch's curse shall be on thee.'

Peter Grimes was a poor man, and the clothes a felon stood in when he died were part of his perquisites, but he had no stomach for a witch's curse, so when he found the gold piece in her shoe as she had promised he took it and was well pleased to leave the worthless chain in place.

She did not die easily, from all accounts. Her splendid body was too powerful, the tide of life ran too strong in her, so she dangled, quivering and writhing in the air a full five minutes. Then Peter Grimes, perhaps in charity, perhaps because he wished to have the business over with and go home to his breakfast, seized her by the legs and dragged until the double burden of his weight and hers proved too much for her spinal column, and with a snapping like the cracking of a fire-dried stick her neck broke and her struggles ended.

They raised the stone that she had set above her husband's empty grave, scooped out a shallow opening beneath it and dropped her in, coffinless and without proper graveclothes. So, as the neighbours sagely said, she had outreached herself and ordered her own tombstone when by her wicked wizardry she had the tidings of her man's death at the instant it occurred.

And here again we're forced to make a choice between the natural and the supernatural. That Kundre should have confessed she was guilty was not particularly important. We know that under heavy mental stress people will accuse themselves of almost any crime. There's hardly a sensational murder case in which the police don't have to deal with numerous entirely innocent self-accusers. That part of it is understandable.

What is more difficult to explain is that at the very moment Peter Grimes broke Kundre's neck the swelling in Abigail Newton's tongue began to subside, and by noon she had entirely regained the power of speech. Indeed, she regained it so fully that within six months she was twice sentenced to the ducking-stool for public scoldings, and finally was forced to stand before the meeting house on the Sabbath with a muzzle on her face and a paper reading 'Common Scold' hung by a string around her neck.

Not the least mystifying thing about the mystery of Kundre Maltby was the way her fortune disappeared. That she and Pela-tiah had been rich was common knowledge, but when the assessors went to her house to take her property in custody they could find nothing of substantial value. Not a single gold or silver coin, nor yet a bit of jewellery could they turn up, though they searched the place from cellar to ridgepole and even knocked down several walls in quest of concealed hiding places. So, balked in the attempt to work a forfeiture of her fortune, they sold the house and land at public vendue, put the proceeds in the town treasury and farmed the children out to be taught useful trades.

Micah was apprenticed at the rope-walk owned by Goodman Richard Belkton, Kundre took her place among the sewing maids of Goodwife Deborah Stiles, and except when they were in school or went, well chaperoned, to divine service at the meeting house, they never saw each other.

Their lot was not a happy one. We all know the sadistic cruelty of the young. The lad who goes to a new school today has a hard time until he's proved himself to be the equal of the class bully, or till the novelty of hazing him wears off. But Kundre and her brother had to face the taunts and insults of their classmates endlessly. No one wished to sit with them or share a hornbook with them. If, maddened by the spiteful things said of his mother, Micah fought his tormentor and came off winner, his victory was vociferously attributed to witchcraft. If he lost the fight the victor called on all to witness how Heaven had helped the right in overcoming evil.

Both were apt pupils, but their readiness in reading, ciphering and writing caused no commendation from the schoolma'am. She too believed their aptitude infernally inspired and made no secret of it. So successful recitations were rewarded by an acid reference to their mother's compact with the Evil One. Failure brought a caning.

In all the dreary monotone of life the one highlight for Kundre was Hosea Newton. It may seem strange that the son of her mother's fiercest persecutor should prove her only friend, but it was no stranger than the contrast between Hosea and his mother. Where she was angular and acid and sharp-tongued he was inclined to plumpness, slow of speech and even-tempered. When all the little girls drew their skirts back from Kundre as from diabolic pollution, he chose a seat beside her on the form, and shared his primer with her and, to the scandal of the class, often gave her tidbits from the ample luncheon which his mother packed for him each morning. When Charity Wilkins accused Kundre of stealing a new thimble from her he found the missing bauble concealed in Charity's pocket and pulled her hair until she admitted her fault. Charity's big brother Benjamin took up the lists for his sister, whereupon Hosea entered combat with enthusiasm and left Benjamin with a bloody nose and greatly chastened tongue.

But this little interlude of friendship had disastrous results. Goodwife Wilkins went to Abigail, who, horrified that her son had espoused the witch-child's cause, took him forthwith to Reverend Silas Middleton, who quoted Scriptual texts to him—'Evil communications corrupt good manners'— exhorted him, prayed over him and finally caned him soundly.

After that Hosea had to content himself with smiling at Kundre over his primer. All speech between them was forbidden, and though the Reverend Middleton's precepts had made but small impression on Hosea, he had a vivid memory of the thrashing that accompanied them.

The quiet of the lazy years flowed over Danby like a placid river. In the harbour the tall ships shook out their wings and sped to the far corners of the earth and presently came back again with holds filled with strange merchandise. Or perhaps they did not come back, and the women put on mourning clothes and there were new stones in the churchyard, with empty graves beneath them. King Philip's War was fought and won and the settlers needed to fear Indian raids no longer. But in the main life just went on and on. Its groove was deepened, but the course and pattern never changed.

Hosea Newton went away to Harvard College where he was to be trained for the ministry, Micah worked at the rope-walk, harbouring black resentment in his heart, but not daring to give tongue to it; Kundre toiled in Goody Stiles's workroom from sunrise to sunset. She proved a clever needle-woman and her work was eagerly bought up, but had no credit for it. Goodwife Stiles displayed the dresses proudly, and accepted compliments with modest grace, but she never told whose agile fingers fashioned them. In this she showed sound business sense, for many of her customers would have hesitated to wear garments made by a witch-child. And then—

One evening in late summer Kundre lay in Goodman Stiles's oat field. She had worked all day, her eyes and muscles ached, and she was so tired that she could have cried with it, but now she had a little respite. The earth felt warm and comforting to her cramped muscles, she seemed to draw vitality from it while a little breeze played through the bearded grain, making it rustle softly, like a bride's dress.

A bride's dress! Kundre thought. Other maids went to the meeting house or stood up in their own homes in stiff, rustling taffety while the parson joined them to the men of their choice. Was she forever doomed to tread the earth in loneliness, to find no lover, no friend, even, in the whole world? It seemed a hard fate for a maid as well-favoured as she.

Kundre knew that she had beauty. Unlike her mother, she was little; little and slender with grey eyes and a soft-lipped, rather sad smile. Her hair, despite the severe braids in which she wore it, was positively thrilling in its beauty. Paler than her mother's, it had the sweet amber-gold of melted honey in dark lights and the vivid sheen of burnished silver when the sunshine fell on it. There was a sort of aristocratic fragility hinted at by her arched, slender neck and delicately-cut profile, her hands were so slight that she wore child's mittens in cold weather, and the cast-off shoon of neighbours' half-grown daughters were too large for her, even when she wore the thickest woollen stockings.

But now she had kicked off the rough brogans and stripped the heavy cotton stockings off and drew her naked, gleaming feet up under her as she half sat, half lay upon the warm and friendly earth. She rested her elbow upon a bent knee, outlining her chin with her fingers as she looked toward the blue, distant hills. How would it seem, she wondered, to have someone look at her in friendship, speak a kindly word to her, perhaps—her pulses quickened at the daring thought—tell her she was beautiful?

A footstep sounded at the margin of the field and she crouched like a little partridge when it hears the hunter coming. If she were very still, perhaps whoever came would pass her by unseeing. She had no wish to be seen. Since early childhood she had never known a friendly look or word, except—

The footsteps came still nearer, swishing through the nodding grain, and now she heard a man's voice humming softly:

Wish and fulfilment can severed be ne'er,
Nor the thing prayed for come short of the prayer—

'I crave thy pardon, mistress!' Unaware of Kundre crouching in her covet he had almost trodden on her. A flush suffused his face as he stepped backward hurriedly and almost lost his balance in the process.

'I had no business trespassing on Neighbour Stiles's land—why, Kundre, lass, is't truly thou? How lovely thou art grown!' he broke off in surprised delight and to her utter blank amazement, dropped down to the ground beside her. 'It must be full three years since I have seen thee,' he added.

Kundre looked at him in wonder. At first it had been but a man she saw, and men, almost as much as women, were her natural enemies, for she had led an odd and hunted life, and like an animal knew the world of men and women only through the blows it dealt her. But as she looked into the smiling friendly face she felt the blood flow into her cheeks and bring sudden warmth to her brow, for it was Hosea Newton sitting by her in the oat field, Hosea Newton's voice, all rich with friendly laughter, asked how she did, and—her heart beat so that she could hardly breathe—Hosea Newton has just said that she was lovely.

The years had been kind to him. Strongly made, wide-shouldered, he was still not burly, only big; and his face was undeniably handsome. He had a short upper lip and a square jaw with a dimple in it, blue eyes set wide apart beneath dark, curving brows, and lightly curling dark hair that fitted his well-formed head like a cap.

'Art glad to see me?' he asked frankly, and Kundre sat in thoughtful silence for a while before she answered softly:

'I am not sure, Hosea. In all the world thou art the only person who has spoken kindly to me since my mother—died—but once, I recollect, thou suffered for thy kindness to me. Now—'

'Now,' he mimicked laughing, 'I'll dare the parson or the elders to admonish me. I am my own man, Kundre, and think what thoughts I choose, say what I will and go with whom I please. Aye,' he added as she answered nothing. 'I've thought a deal about things, Kundre, and what I think might not make pleasant hearing for the parson and the elders, or my mother, either. I've seen the Quakers whipped and hanged and branded for their faith's sake, seen helpless, innocent old women go tottering to the gallows tree for witchcraft that they never worked, and could not work, and seen the men who call themselves God's ministers work lustily in Satan's vineyard.'

'Thou thinkest, then—' she asked him with a quaver in her voice—'it may be possible my mother was no witch—'

'No more a witch than any other,' he replied. 'Though I speak of the flesh that bore me, I say that those who swore her life away are tainted with the blood of innocence—why, Kundre, lass, what aileth thee?'

The girl had flung her arms about him and was sobbing out her heart against his shoulder. For almost twenty years she'd led a pariah's life, hounded, scorned and persecuted, and the memory of her mother had been rubbed into her breaking heart like salt in a raw wound. Now here at last was one who had a kind word for her mother, who dared suggest she had not merited a felon's shameful death.

What happened then was like a chemical reaction in its spontaneity. It may have been that pity which is said to be akin to love inspired him to put his arms about her as she sobbed against his shoulder, but in the fraction of a heart-beat there was no questioning the emotion that possessed him. From him to her, and from her to him, there seemed to flow a mystic fluid—a sort of intangible soul-substance—that met and mingled like the waters of two rivers at their confluence and merged them into each other until they were not twain, but one.

It was an odd idyll, this romance of a man whose childhood had been spent in the house with a bawling woman and this woman whose whole life had been warped by hatred and suspicion. To say that they loved at first sight would not be accurate. Each had carried the image of the other in his heart since childhood, in each the thought of the other had been present constantly, not consciously, any more than they were conscious of the hearts that beat beneath their breasts, but always there, the greatest, most important, most vital thing in either of their lives. Now they were aware of it with blinding, dazzling suddenness. The glory of it almost stunned them.

Every evening when her work for Goody Stiles was done Kundre hurried to the oat field, and always he was there to greet her and come hurrying with uplifted hands to take her in his arms.

Judged by modern free-and-easy standards they were inhibited in their love-making. They hardly kissed at all, and when they did it was a chaste embrace which brother and sister might have exchanged. But she would put her hand in his and turn it till her soft palm rested on his and her little fingers made a soft and gentle pattern of his own, then rest her head against his shoulder till her gleaming hair was on his cheek, its perfume fresh and sweet as that of the green growing things about them.

I said theirs was an odd love. So it was. A love compounded partly of loneliness, partly of heart-hunger, partly of true, honest friendship; not without its moments of passion, but entirely without the savage, selfish hunger of passion; not lacking ecstasy, but with the ecstasy of love fulfilled, not satiated.

They did not talk much. There was small need of words, for that mysterious warm current, strong as a rising ocean tide, flowed constantly between them, fusing their two selves in one.

And when they came to say good night the sweet pain of their parting was itself a compensation for the day-long separation facing them.

Then came catastrophe, as dreadful and as unexpected as a thunder-bolt hurled from a cloudless sky. Her brother Micah ran away from his master. It was either flight or murder, for despite the expert way in which he did his work old Goodman Belkton found fault with him constantly, and his fellow 'prentices, not slow to take their cue from the master, taunted him with his mother's conviction and intimated that he used her devilish arts to make his handiwork the best the 'walk turned out.

Runaway apprentices were fair game for anyone, and Goodman Belkton offered a reward of two pounds for the stray's return, so when four sturdy louts saw Micah on the dock at Salem Town, about to sign before the mast for a voyage in the Indies, they set on him and bound him with a length of rope and dragged him back to Danby.

But while they were still in the Danby suburbs they had been set upon by a ferocious heifer that gored one of them sorely, knocked down another, and put them all so utterly to flight that their prisoner escaped and joined his ship at Salem before she sailed with the tide. They brought their wounded comrade into Danby, where, over sundry mugs of potent rum-and-water, they had a wondrous story to relate.

The cow that set on them had been no ordinary cow, it seemed, but a demon beast whose nostrils breathed forth fiery flames, and which announced *in human words*, 'I'll soon set thee free from this scum, my brother!'

This all happened in the early evening, but before it was too dark for them to see the demon beast go tearing off across a meadow when its fell work had been done and suddenly sit down upon the sod like a woman, straddle a long fence-rail like a witch that mounts a broom, and fly shrieking off across the sky toward Goodman Stiles's oat field.

And where had Kundre been while this was happening? Her mistress asked her pointblank, and pointblank she refused to answer. And there the matter might have rested, perhaps, if Jonathan Sawyer, a labourer of Goodman Williams' plantation, had not volunteered the information that at nine o'clock the night before he's seen her hurrying from Stiles's oat field and heard her singing something not to be found in the hymn book.

It seemed hardly necessary for the constable to call a *posse comitans* of trained bandsmen to arrest her or to summon Parson Middleton to lend them spiritual assistance. But so he did, and with martial clank of sword and pike and musket, and with the Parson with his Book beneath his arm, they went to Goodwife Stiles's house and formally took Kundre into custody, bound her wrists together with the constable's spare bridle, put a horse's leading-strap about her neck and marched her through the streets to Danby jail, where they lodged her with a double guard before the door.

Hosea Newton roused from a deep, dream-tormented sleep, completely conscious, every faculty alert. His room was buried in a darkness blinding as a black cloak, for the moon had set long since, and a cloud-veil obscured the stars. Some instinct, some sentinel of the spirit that stands watch while we are sleeping, told him he was not alone, but he could see or hear nothing.

All day he'd raged through Danby Town like a madman, calling on the parson and the constable and even the high magistrate to intercede for Kundre. She was no witch, he vowed, but a sweet, pure maid who held his heart in the cupped palms of her two little hands. The ruffians who had told the story of the demon heifer were a lot of drunken, craven liars, seeking to excuse their prisoner's escape with this wild tale. He'd prove it; he would range the countryside until he'd found the cow that bested them and lead her singlehanded to the pound for all to see she was a natural beast.

The parson and the constable and magistrate were sympathetic listeners, but one and all refused to help in his trouble. The woman was a witch, the vowed and dedicated votary of Satan—like mother, like daughter. Could any natural cow put four strong men to flight, and they all armed with stout cudgels? And, most especially, could a natural beast bestride a fence-rail and sail through the sky on it? 'Poor boy, thou art bewitched by this vile whelp from Satan's kennels,' they told him.

'But fear not, poor, befuddled lad, tomorrow we shall prove that thy infatuation is the devil's work, for on the town common at sunrise we shall prick the witchling with long pins until we find the devil's mark, and thou shalt see she is in very truth a servant of the Prince of Darkness.'

He'd tried to see her in the jail, but the trained bandsmen turned him back. No one must see the witch until she had passed through the ordeal, even the turnkey was forbidden to go near her or to look into her cell. How should she eat and wherewith should she quench her thirst? Let Beelzebub her master see to that. They were Christian men and had no traffic with the servants of Satan.

Finally, worn out in body and in spirit, he had come home, refused his supper—could he take food while Kundre starved?—and thrown himself upon his bed, full-dressed, to fall into a sleep of utter exhaustion.

Desperate men make desperate plans, and Hosea was desperate. It did not matter to him whether she were good of bad or innocent or guilty. He loved her and would not desert her. If the court found her guilty—and accusation was equivalent to conviction—he would denounce himself as a wizard, and hang with her upon the gallows tree. She should not go to that dark land beyond the grave alone.

What was it? Something stirred in the soft darkness of the room; a shadow moving in the shadows, a rat that came to forage in the dark?

He knew that it was none of these, for in the gloom that blotted out the outlines of the furniture he saw a gleam of light, or rather lightness, like a cloud of faintly luminous vapour swirling from an unseen boiling kettle.

Slowly it spread, wafting upward, and now he saw the outlines of a figure in it, and the blood churned in his ears, his throat grew tight, and at the pit of his stomach he seemed to feel a burning and a freezing, all at once.

'Who—what art thou?' he croaked hoarsely, and the sound of his own frightened voice was terrifying in the haunted darkness.

No answer came to his challenge, but the figure looming faintly in the mist-cloud seemed taking on a kind of substance. Now he could see it quite clearly, and the terror which engulfed him seemed to be an icy flood that paralyzed his heart and brain and muscles.

Yet notwithstanding his terror he felt a kind of admiration for the phantom. It was a woman, tall as a tall man, yet with a calm and regal beauty wholly feminine. Across the low white brow a spate of gold-hued hair fell flowing to her knees, and from the perfect contour of her face great eyes of zenith-blue looked at him under brows of startling blackness. She was dressed in widow's weeds: a chain and pendant of some dull, lack-lustre metal hung about her throat.

He knew her! He has been a little lad scarce eight years old when Goodman Stiles had raised him to his shoulder that he might see the hangman Peter Grimes work the court's sentence on Kundre Maltby, the witch-woman. With a sudden pang of recollection he recalled how he had thought it a great pity that so much beauty should be vowed to Satan and hanged upon the gallows tree and entombed in the earth.

'What—' by supreme effort he forced speech between palsied lips—'what wouldst thou with me, Kundre Maltby?'

'Wilt take my help, Hosea Newton?' asked the spectre, and her voice was cold and desolate as December storm-wind blowing over pine-capped hills.

Hosea hesitated in his answer, and well he might. The wraith, if wraith it were, was that of a condemned witch-woman, hanged for sorcery, and, presumably, made fast in hell. He might have been in advance of his time, but he was part and parcel of his generation, and since Deuteronomy was penned men had regarded witches as disciples of the Evil One. To traffic with them was forbidden under pain of death and loss of soul. This was a witch's ghost, as dreadful as the witch herself, perhaps more dreadful, since she had burned in hell for twenty years, and he must make the choice of taking aid from her or bidding her begone. There was no middle course; he must hold true to all the teachings that had been instilled in him since infancy and bid her avaunt, or make compromise with Evil incarnate and put his soul in dreadful jeopardy—to what end? Did not the writings of the Fathers teach that Satan is the arch-deceiver? Would he keep the compact offered by this messenger from hell?

Then came the thought of Kundre, little Kundre, starved and thirsting, languishing in prison till the morrow, when they'd strip her to her shift in sight of all the town and pierce her tender flesh with long, cruel pins—a thousand thousand years of burning hell would be a bargain-price to pay for her deliverance.

'Say on, O spirit of my Kundre's mother,' he commanded. 'I'll take the help thou offerest me, and pay the price thou asketh.'

The phantom raised one white, almost transparent hand and loosed the medal from its neck. 'Take this,' it bade, and it seemed that its ghostly voice was stronger, warmer. 'Hie with it to the jail house and cut away the bars that pen her in. Then fly across the border southward—my time is sped, I must e'en go!'

The voice stopped suddenly, as though a hand had been laid on the spectre's throat, and like an April snowflake melting in the rising sun of spring, the faintly-shining vision merged back in the darkness.

He could not say if it had been a vivid dream or if a visitant had come to him, but presently he rose and struck a flint-spark in his tinderbox and lit a tallow dip. There on the floor beside his bed lay a medallion of dull metal, not lead nor iron, but apparently a mixture of the two, fixed to a length of slender chain of the same sheenless substance. Curiously, he noted that his hands were soiled with fresh earth and his fingernails broken, as though he had been burrowing like a woodchuck. Yet he knew he had not left his chamber since he flung himself upon the bed and fell asleep.

Or had he? We may wonder. Might he not have been the victim of somnambulism, and risen to go scraping at the earth that covered Kundre Maltby's body in the churchyard, then, still asleep, come back with the mysterious medal? The thought did not occur to him, but in the light of modern psychological experiments we may entertain it.

At any rate he recognized the medallion and took it in his hand. It was quite plain on one side and engraved with characters he could not read upon the other. Its edge was rounded like that of a milled coin, and though it was no larger than a penny it weighed as much as a gold sovereign.

What was it that the ghost had ordered him to do? Hie with it to the jail house and cut away the bars that pen her in.'

With this dull piece of soft metal? He was about to fling the medal from him in disgust when the echo of the ghostly voice seemed coming to him through the candlelight-stained darkness. 'Hurry, hurry, lover of the falsely-accused, or it will be too late!'

He knew what cell they'd lodged her in, the same in which her mother languished twenty years ago. It was on the ground floor of the prison, and by standing on his tiptoes he could look through the barred window.

If they caught him skulking round the jail house—What matter? He was resolved to die with her, why not share prison with her ere they hanged him?

Danby jail loomed dimly, a darker darkness in the starless night, as Hosea approached it, treading noiselessly in stockinged feet. 'Kundre,' he whispered softly as he tapped upon the stone sill of her cell window. 'Can'st hear me, dearest love?'

'Is't thou, my very dearest?' the girl's reply came to him through the formless darkness. 'Oh, Hosea—' He heard her sobs, the small, sad sounds of utter misery, as her voice broke.

'Aye, heart o' mine, 'tis I, and I have come to tell thee that thou shalt not go alone—come closer, love, stretch out thy hands to me—'

'I cannot, dearest one; they've chained me to the wall as if I were a rabid cur—'

Hosea clenched his teeth in fury and, unthinking, drove his hand against the prison bars. It was the hand in which he clasped the witch's medal, and as it struck the bar he drew back with a startled exclamation. The heavy, hand-forged iron had melted from contact with the medal as if it had been tallow touched by flame.

In a moment he was sawing at the window-bars with the mysterious coin, cutting them away as if they had been cheese. Silently he laid them on the turf outside the prison window, then, when he had an opening large enough to crawl through, let himself inside the cell and felt his way toward her.

They wasted no time in reunion or premature rejoicings. With her hand on his to guide it he pressed the witch's coin against the iron collar locked around her neck, and laid the fetter on the straw-strewn cell floor carefully, lest its clanking rouse the guard who waited in the corridor outside. Then, step by cautious step, he led her to the window.

Hand in hand they crept along the shadowed street until they reached the stable where his mother's horses stamped before their mangers. In a moment he had saddled the best beast and led it out, swung her to the saddle-bow before him and set out toward the southern boundary of the town. They dared not trot or gallop lest the pounding of the horse's hoofs arouse the neighbours, but presently they reached the churchyard, and he drove his heels into the stallion's flanks.

'Wait, wait, my dear,' she begged him as they passed the white-spired meeting house, 'I would say farewell to my mother ere we shake the dust of Danby from our shoon forever.'

'Aye,' he conceded, lowering her to the ground. 'That is but fitting, sweetling. We are indebted to thy mother for thy liberty tonight.'

Together they walked to the grave, and while the girl knelt on the moss that rimmed the stone he looked down at her pensively. He wondered why his conscience did not trouble him. Tonight he had accepted diabolic aid, made compromise with Evil. Even now he had the witch-wife's medal in his pocket—he drew the flat metallic disc to look at it. Should he take it with him, or return it to the grave? he wondered, then wondered more at what was happening. The coin seem straining at his fingers, as if a thin, invisible thread were pulling it, or it had volition of its own and sought release from his grasp.

But, strangely, the pull was all in one direction, toward the foot of Kundre Maltby's grave.

Wonderingly, he stepped in the direction of the tug, and noticed that it increased sharply, then seemed to bear straight down toward the earth.

He dropped upon his knees. The coin seemed guiding his hand toward the tombstone and, still marvelling, he reached in the direction that it indicated. His fingers touched the long grass growing by the stone and found an opening like a woodchuck's burrow. Inside was something stiff and hard, yet slightly pliable, like old, oiled leather.

He grasped the object, tugged at it and brought it out. It was a leather sack, well smeared with tallow, stiff with age and long entombment in the earth, but wholly intact. A wax seal held the cord that bound its mouth, but this crumbled as he touched it. Inside were several smaller sacks, some of soft buckskin, some of coarse linen, and in them were bright English sovereigns, round silver Spanish dollars, and gleaming articles of jewellery. The mystery of Kundre Maltby's lost fortune was solved. She had buried it beneath the stone that marked her husband's empty grave, and when they went to scoop the hollow to receive her body they had used only the upper portion of the grave.

Hosea chuckled as he realized what has happened. The diggers' spades had been within a hand's-width of the treasure, yet none had suspected it.

Witchcraft? Perhaps, but very fortunate witchcraft for him and Kundre. A moment since they had had nothing but the clothes they stood in and the stolen stallion; now they were rich. Their life would not be hard—if they could get away.

The night was tiring rapidly as they rode into the woodland. Long streaks of grey were showing in the eastern sky, small noises came to them, the chirp of crickets and the sleepy murmurs of awakening birds, but on and on they rode, secure in the knowledge that Danby jail had no bloodhounds to pursue them, and their escape could not be known till sunrise, for no one, jailer or turnkey or guard, would dare go near the witch's cell till full daylight.

The Newport Quakers greeted them hospitably, and when they found that they had money offered them letters to the first citizens of Philadelphia.

In two days they took passage on a sloop bound for the Delaware, and, once on the high sea, were married by the master. So Kundre Maltby and Hosea Newton, children of seafaring Danby skippers, plighted troth upon the ocean, with the singing of the wind in the rigging for wedding march and the skirling mewl of sea gulls for a prothalamium.

They were not the first, nor, unhappily, the last to be driven from their homes by ignorance and bigotry masquerading as religion, but in Philadelphia they found such peace and happiness as never could have been theirs in New England. Their house stood on a tall hill overlooking the wide Schuylkill and the prosperous little Quaker city, and there their family multiplied until they had four sons and three daughters.

It was an evening in mid-April, the anniversary of her father's death at Captain Newton's hand, if she had known it, that Kundre stood with Hosea on the porch of their mansion and watched the lights of Philadelphia quench out against the darkness. Honora, their last-born daughter, had been christened in the afternoon, and now, all vestige of original sin washed from her, was slumbering as peacefully as any cherub in the nursery.

'Look, heart of mine,' bade Kundre, 'all those good folk go to their rest down yonder. They are a kind and gentle people, and I know their dreams are of a better world.'

'Aye, dearest,' he slipped an arm round her, 'a better world, in truth. Not in some dim, misty Promised Land on t'other side of Jordan, but here in this same world we live in. There'll come a time, my sweet, when men with lofty dreams shall waken at a great tomorrow's dawn and find their dreams still there, and nothing vanished but the night.'

The Bishop brought his story to a close and looked from Dr Bentley to the younger clergyman with a quizzical twinkle in his eye. 'I shan't ask you to pass judgement,' he said. 'Whether Hosea Newton should have scorned the witch's offer—or whether he received it, for that matter—are purely academic questions today. I'm pretty sure though,' he chuckled, 'that if he had refused it I should not be here this evening.'

'How's that, sir?' asked young Dr Kitteringson.

'Well, you see, Hosea Newton was my great-grandfather, several times removed, and his wife, the witch's child, my ancestress. So was the witch, for that matter.'

'And the witch's coin?' asked Dr Kitteringson. 'Do you know what became of it?'

'Yes,' answered Bishop Chauncey. 'Here it is.' He thrust two fingers in his waistcoat and produced a little metal disc which might have been silver, but it wasn't, flat and plain on one side, marked with faint traces of old Nordic runes upon the other. 'I've carried it as a lucky piece for years,' he added. 'My grandfather carried it all through the Civil War and never had a wound; my father had it with him at San Juan Hill and came off without a scratch. I lugged it through the Argonne and came out safely, but once when I left it on my dressing table in Paris I was run down by a taxi-cab before I had a chance to cross the street.'

Dr. Kitteringson was handling the strange coin gingerly, half curiously, half fearfully. 'You've tested it for magic powers?' he asked.

'Good gracious, no son. I don't suppose it has any, and—good heavens, look!'

Young Dr. Kitteringson had taken up the fire shovel and drawn the coin's blunt edge across its gleaming brass bowl. Where the medal touched the brass it cut a kerf as easily as if it had been pressed through softened tallow.

'Great Scott, Bishop—Dick!' exclaimed Dr Bentley. 'What do you think of that?'

The Bishop dropped the witch's coin back in his waistcoat pocket and held his glass out toward his host. His hand was shaking slightly, but his eyes and voice were steady. 'I think I'd like another drop of brandy; quickly, if you please,' he answered.

AUTHOR'S NOTE

Is the Devil a Gentleman? is a question story. Whether Kundre Maltby was a witch at all, whether she appeared as a ghost to her future son-in-law, whether he actually compromised with evil or whether he was the victim of a vivid dream and a case of somnambulism—all these are questions which are continually raised through the course of the story.

Like an advocate, I've merely presented the evidence in the case, but unlike an advocate, I've forborn to argue from the evidence; hence the jury of readers must reach their verdict without help or hints from me.

Background for the story : Turn to page 117 of the Cambridge edition of the poems of John Greenleaf Whittier. There it all is, beautifully outlined for you, except for the Bishop, and the witch's coin and a few little things which I thought up myself.

SEABURY QUINN

YOUNG GOODMAN BROWN

by Nathaniel Hawthorne

YOUNG Goodman Brown came forth at sunset into the street of Salem village; but put his head back, after crossing the threshold, to exchange a parting kiss with his young wife. And Faith, as the wife was aptly named, thrust her own pretty head into the street, letting the wind play with the pink ribbons of her cap while she called to Goodman Brown.

"Dearest heart," whispered she, softly and rather sadly, when her lips were close to his ear, "prithee put off your journey until sunrise and sleep in your own bed tonight. A lone woman is troubled with such dreams and such thoughts that she's afeared of herself sometimes. Pray tarry with me this night, dear husband, of all nights in the year."

"My love and my Faith," replied young Goodman Brown, "of all nights in the year, this one night must I tarry away from thee. My journey, as thou callest it, forth and back again, must needs be done 'twixt now and sunrise. What, my sweet, pretty wife, dost thou doubt me already, and we but three months married?"

"Then God bless you!" said Faith, with the pink ribbons; "and may you find all well when you come back."

"Amen!" cried Goodman Brown. "Say thy prayers, dear Faith, and go to bed at dusk, and no harm will come to thee."

So they parted; and the young man pursued his way until,

being about to turn the corner by the meeting-house, he looked back and saw the head of Faith still peeping after him with a melancholy air, in spite of her pink ribbons.

"Poor little Faith!" thought he, for his heart smote him. "What a wretch am I to leave her on such an errand! She talks of dreams, too. Methought as she spoke, there was trouble in her face, as if a dream had warned her what work is to be done tonight. But no, no; 'twould kill her to think it. Well, she's a blessed angel on earth; and after this one night I'll cling to her skirts and follow her to heaven."

With this excellent resolve for the future, Goodman Brown felt himself justified in making more haste on his present evil purpose. He had taken a dreary road, darkened by all the gloomiest trees of the forest, which barely stood aside to let the narrow path creep through, and closed immediately behind. It was all as lonely as could be; and there is this peculiarity in such a solitude, that the traveller knows not who may be concealed by the innumerable trunks and the thick boughs overhead; so that with lonely footsteps he may yet be passing through an unseen multitude.

"There may be a devilish Indian behind every tree," said Goodman Brown to himself; and he glanced fearfully behind him as he added, "What if the Devil himself should be at my very elbow!"

His head being turned back, he passed a crook of the road, and, looking forward again, beheld the figure of a man, in grave and decent attire, seated at the foot of an old tree. He arose at Goodman Brown's approach and walked onward side by side with him.

"You are late, Goodman Brown," said he. "The clock of the Old South was striking as I came through Boston; and that is full fifteen minutes agone."

"Faith kept me back awhile," replied the young man, with a tremor in his voice, caused by the sudden appearance of his companion, though not wholly unexpected.

It was now deep dusk in the forest, and deepest in that

part of it where these two were journeying. As nearly as could be discerned, the second traveller was about fifty years old, apparently in the same rank of life as Goodman Brown, and bearing a considerable resemblance to him, though perhaps more in expression than features. Still they might have been taken for father and son. And yet, though the elder person was as simply clad as the younger and as simple in manner too, he had an indescribable air of one who knew the world, and who would not have felt abashed at the governor's dinner-table or in King William's court, were it possible that his affairs should call him thither. But the only thing about him that could be fixed upon as remarkable was his staff, which bore the likeness of a great black snake, so curiously wrought that it might almost be seen to twist and wriggle itself like a living serpent. This, of course, must have been an ocular deception, assisted by the uncertain light.

"Come, Goodman Brown," cried his fellow-traveller, "this is a dull pace for the beginning of a journey. Take my staff, if you are so soon weary."

"Friend," said the other, exchanging his slow pace for a full stop, "having kept covenant by meeting thee here, it is my purpose now to return whence I came. I have scruples touching the matter thou wot'st of."

"Sayest thou so?" replied he of the serpent, smiling apart. "Let us walk on, nevertheless, reasoning as we go; and if I convince thee not, thou shalt turn back. We are but a little way in the forest yet."

"Too far! Too far!" exclaimed the goodman, unconsciously resuming his walk. "My father never went into the woods on such an errand, nor his father before him. We have been a race of honest men and good Christians since the days of the martyrs; and shall I be the first by the name of Brown that ever took this path and kept – "

"Such company, thou wouldn't say," observed the elder person, interpreting his pause. "Well said, Goodman Brown! I have been as well acquainted with your family as with ever a one among the Puritans; and that's no trifle to say. I helped your grandfather, the constable, when he lashed the Quaker woman so smartly through the streets of Salem; and it was I that brought your father a pitch-pine knot, kindled at my own hearth, to set fire to an Indian village, in King Philip's war. They were my good friends both; and many a pleasant walk have we had along this path, and returned merrily after midnight. I would fain be friends with you for their sake."

"If it be as thou sayest," replied Goodman Brown, "I marvel they never spoke of these matters; or, verily, I marvel not, seeing that the least rumour of the sort would have driven them from New England. We are a people of prayer, and good works to boot, and abide no such wickedness."

"Wickedness or not," said the traveller with the twisted staff, "I have a very general acquaintance here in New England. The deacons of many a church have drunk the communion wine with me; the select men of divers towns make me their chairman; and a majority of the Great and General Court are firm supporters of my interests. The governor and I, too – these are state secrets."

"Can this be so?" cried Goodman Brown, with a stare of amazement at his undisturbed companion. "Howbeit, I have nothing to do with the governor and council; they have their own ways, and are no rule for a simple husbandman like me. But, were I to go on with thee, how should I meet the eye of that good old man, our minister, at Salem village? Oh, his voice would make me tremble both Sabbath day and lecture day!"

Thus far the elder traveller had listened with due gravity; but now burst into a fit of irrepressible mirth, shaking himself so violently that his snake-like staff actually seemed to wriggle in sympathy.

"Ha! ha! ha!" shouted he again and again; then composing himself, "Well, go on, Goodman Brown, go on; but, prithee, don't kill me with laughing."

"Well, then, to end the matter at once," said Goodman Brown, considerably nettled, "there is my wife, Faith. It would break her dear little heart, and I'd rather break my own."

"Nay, if that be the case," answered the other, "e'en go thy ways, Goodman Brown. I would not for twenty old women like the one hobbling before us that Faith should come to any harm."

As he spoke, he pointed his staff at a female figure on the path, in whom Goodman Brown recognized a very pious and exemplary dame, who had taught him his catechism in youth, and was still his moral and spiritual adviser, jointly with the minister and Deacon Gookin.

"A marvel, truly, that Goody Cloyse should be so far in the wilderness at nightfall," said he. "But, with your leave, friend, I shall take a cut through the woods until we have left this Christian woman behind. Being a stranger to you, she might ask whom I was consorting with and whither I was going."

"Be it so," said his fellow-traveller. "Betake you to the woods, and let me keep the path."

Accordingly the young man turned aside, but took care to watch his companion, who advanced softly along the road until he had come within a staff's length of the old dame. She, meanwhile, was making the best of her way, with singular speed for so aged a woman, and mumbling some indistinct words – a prayer, doubtless – as she went. The traveller put forth his staff and touched her withered neck with what seemed the serpent's tail.

"The Devil!" screamed the pious old lady.

"Then Goody Cloyse knows her old friend?" observed the traveller, confronting her and leaning on his writhing stick.

"Ah, forsooth, and is it your worship indeed?" cried the

good old dame. "Yea, truly is it, and in the very image of my old gossip, Goodman Brown, the grandfather of the silly fellow that now is. But – would your worship believe it? – my broomstick hath strangely disappeared, stolen as I suspect, by that unhanged witch, Goody Cory, and that, too, when I was all anointed with the juice of smallage, and cinquefoil, and wolf's-bane – "

"Mingled with fine wheat and the fat of a new-born babe," said the shape of old Goodman Brown.

"Ah, your worship knows the recipe," cried the old lady, cackling aloud. "So, as I was saying, being all ready for the meeting, and no horse to ride on, I made up my mind to foot it; for they tell me there is a nice young man to be taken into communion tonight. But now your good worship will lend me your arm, and we shall be there in a twinkling."

"That can hardly be," answered her friend. "I may not spare you my arm, Goody Cloyse; but here is my staff, if you will."

So saying, he threw it down at her feet, where, perhaps, it assumed life, being one of the rods which its owner had formerly lent to the Egyptian magi. Of this fact, however, Goodman Brown could not take cognizance. He had cast up his eyes in astonishment, and looking down again, beheld neither Goody Cloyse nor the serpentine staff, but his fellow-traveller alone, who waited for him as calmly as if nothing had happened.

"That old woman taught me my catechism," said the young man; and there was a world of meaning in this simple comment.

They continued to walk onward, while the elder traveller exhorted his companion to make good speed and persevere in the path, discoursing so aptly that his arguments seemed rather to spring up in the bosom of his auditor than to be suggested by himself. As they went, he plucked a branch of maple to serve for a walking-stick, and began to strip it of the twigs and little boughs, which were wet with evening dew. The moment his fingers touched them they became strangely withered and dried up as with a week's sunshine. Thus the pair proceeded, at a good free pace, until suddenly, in a gloomy hollow of the road, Goodman Brown sat himself down on the stump of a tree and refused to go any farther.

"Friend," said he, stubbornly, "my mind is made up. Not another step will I budge on this errand. What if a wretched old woman do choose to go to the Devil when I thought she was going to heaven : is that any reason why I should quit my dear Faith and go after her?"

"You will think better of this by and by," said his acquaintance, composedly. "Sit here and rest yourself awhile; and when you feel like moving again, there's my staff to help you along."

Without more words, he threw his companion the maple-stick, and was as speedily out of sight as if he had vanished into the deepening gloom. The young man sat a few moments by the roadside, applauding himself greatly and thinking with how clear a conscience he should meet the minister in his morning walk, nor shrink from the eye of good old Deacon Gookin. And what calm sleep would be his that very night, which was to have been spent so wickedly, but so purely and sweetly now, in the arms of Faith! Amidst these pleasant and praiseworthy meditations, Goodman Brown heard the tramp of horses along the road, and deemed it advisable to conceal himself within the verge of the forest, conscious of the guilty purpose that had brought him thither, though now so happily turned from it.

On came the hoof-tramps and the voices of the riders, two grave old voices, conversing soberly as they drew near. These mingled sounds appeared to pass along the road, within a few yards of the young man's hiding-place; but, owing doubtless to the depth of the gloom at that particular spot, neither the travellers nor their steeds were visible. Though their figures brushed the small boughs by the wayside, it could not be seen that they intercepted, even for a moment, the faint gleam from the strip of bright sky athwart which they must have passed. Goodman Brown alternately crouched and stood on tiptoe, pulling aside the branches and thrusting forth his head as far as he durst, without discerning so much as a shadow. It vexed him the more, because he could have sworn, were such a thing possible, that he recognized the voices of the minister and Deacon Gookin, jogging along quietly, as they were wont to do, when bound to some ordination or ecclesiastical council. While yet within hearing, one of the riders stopped to pluck a switch.

"Of the two, reverend sir," said the voice like the deacon's, "I had rather miss an ordination dinner than tonight's meeting. They tell me that some of our community are to be here from Falmouth and beyond, and others from Connecticut and Rhode Island, besides several of the Indian pow-wows, who, after their fashion, know almost as much devilry as the best of us. Moreover, there is a goodly young woman to be taken into communion."

"Mighty well, Deacon Gookin!" replied the solemn old tones of the minister. "Spur up, or we shall be late. Nothing can be done, you know, until I get on the ground."

The hoofs clattered again; and the voices, talking so strangely in the empty air, passed on through the forest, where no church had ever been gathered or solitary Christian prayed. Whither, then, could these holy men be journeying so deep into the heathen wilderness? Young Goodman Brown caught hold of a tree for support, being ready to sink down on the ground, faint and overburdened with the heavy sickness of his heart. He looked up to the sky, doubting whether there really was a heaven above him. Yet there was the blue arch, and the stars brightening in it.

"With heaven above and Faith below, I will yet stand firm against the Devil!" cried Goodman Brown.

While he still gazed upward into the deep arch of the firmament and had lifted his hands to pray, a cloud, though no wind was stirring, hurried across the zenith and hid the brightening stars. The blue sky was still visible except directly overhead, where this black mass of cloud was sweeping swiftly northward. Aloft in the air, as if from the depths of the cloud, came a confused and doubtful sound of voices. Once the listener fancied that he could distinguish the accents of townspeople of his own, men and women, both pious and ungodly, many of whom he had met at the communion-table, and had seen others rioting at the tavern. The next moment, so indistinct were the sounds, he doubted whether he had heard aught but the murmur of the old forest, whispering without a wind. Then came a stronger swell of those familiar tones, heard daily in the sunshine at Salem village, but never until now from a cloud of night. There was one voice, of a young woman, uttering lamentations, yet with an uncertain sorrow, and entreating for some favour, which, perhaps, it would grieve her to obtain; and all the unseen multitudes, both saints and sinners, seemed to encourage her onward.

"Faith!" shouted Goodman Brown, in a voice of agony and desperation; and the echoes of the forest mocked him, crying, "Faith! Faith!" as if bewildered wretches were seeking her all through the wilderness.

The cry of grief, rage, and terror was yet piercing the night, when the unhappy husband held his breath for a response. There was a scream, drowned immediately in a louder murmur of voices, fading into far-off laughter, as the dark cloud swept away, leaving the clear and silent sky above Goodman Brown. But something fluttered lightly down through the air and caught on the branch of a tree. The young man seized it, and beheld a pink ribbon.

"My Faith is gone!" cried he, after one stupefied moment. "There is no good on earth; and sin is but a name. Come, Devil; for to thee is this world given."

And, maddened with despair, so that he laughed loud and long, did Goodman Brown grasp his staff and set forth again, at such a rate that he seemed to fly along the forest path rather than to walk or run. The road grew wilder and drearier and more faintly traced, and vanished at length, leaving him in the heart of the dark wilderness, still rushing onward with the instinct that guides mortal man to evil. The whole forest was peopled with frightful sounds – the creaking of the trees, the howling of wild beasts, and the yell of Indians; while sometimes the wind tolled like a distant church-bell, and sometimes gave a broad roar around the traveller, as if all Nature were laughing him to scorn. But he was himself the chief horror of the scene, and shrank not from its other horrors.

"Ha! ha! ha!" roared Goodman Brown when the wind laughed at him. "Let us hear which will laugh loudest. Think not to frighten me with your devilry. Come witch, come wizard, come Indian pow-wow, come Devil himself, and here comes Goodman Brown. You may as well fear him as he fears you."

In truth, all through the haunted forest there could be nothing more frightful than the figure of Goodman Brown. On he flew among the black pines, brandishing his staff with frenzied gestures, now giving vent to an inspiration of horrid blasphemy, and now shouting forth such laughter as set all the echoes of the forest laughing like demons around him. The fiend in his own shape is less hideous than when he rages in the breast of man. Thus sped the demoniac on his course, until, quivering among the trees, he saw a red light before him, as when the felled trunks and branches of a clearing have been set on fire, and throw up their lurid blaze against the sky, at the hour of midnight. He paused, in a lull of the tempest that had driven him onward, and heard the swell of what seemed a hymn rolling solemnly from a distance with the weight of many voices. He knew the tune; it was a familiar one in the choir of the village meeting-house. The verse died heavily away, and was lengthened by a chorus, not of human voices, but of all the sounds of the benighted wilderness pealing in awful harmony together. Goodman Brown cried out; and his cry was lost to his own ear by its unison with the cry of the desert.

In the interval of silence he stole forward until the light glared full upon his eyes. At one extremity of an open space, hemmed in by the dark wall of the forest, arose a rock, bearing some rude, natural resemblance either to an altar or a pulpit and surrounded by four blazing pines, their tops aflame, their stems untouched, like candles at an evening meeting. The mass of foliage that had overgrown the summit of the rock was all on fire, blazing high into the night and fitfully illuminating the whole field. Each pendent twig and leafy festoon was in a blaze. As the red light arose and fell, a numerous congregation alternately shone forth, then disappeared in shadow, and again grew, as it were, out of the darkness, peopling the heart of the solitary woods at once.

"A grave and dark-clad company," quoth Goodman Brown.

In truth they were such. Among them, quivering to and fro between gloom and splendour, appeared faces that would be seen next day at the council board of the province, and others which, Sabbath after Sabbath, looked devoutly heavenward, and benignantly over the crowded pews, from the holiest pulpits in the land. Some affirmed that the lady of the governor was there. At least there were high dames well known to her, and wives of honoured husbands, and widows, a great multitude, and ancient maidens, all of excellent repute, and fair young girls, who trembled lest their mothers should espy them. Either the sudden gleams of light flashing over the obscure field bedazzled Goodman Brown, or he recognized a score of the church-members of Salem village famous for their especial sanctity. Good old Deacon Gookin had arrived, and waited at the skirts of that venerable saint, his revered pastor. But, irreverently consorting with these grave, reputable, and pious people, these elders of the church, these chaste dames and dewy virgins, there were men of dissolute lives and women of spotted fame, wretches given over to all mean and filthy vice, and suspected even of horrid crimes. It was strange to see that the good shrank not from the wicked, nor were the sinners abashed by the saints. Scattered also among their pale-faced enemies were the Indian priests, or pow-wows, who had often scared their native forest with more hideous incantations than any known to English witchcraft.

"But where is Faith?" thought Goodman Brown; and, as hope came into his heart, he trembled.

Another verse of the hymn arose, a slow and mournful strain, such as the pious love, but joined to words which expressed all that our nature can conceive of sin, and darkly hinted at far more. Unfathomable to mere mortals is the lore of fiends. Verse after verse was sung; and still the chorus of the desert swelled between like the deepest tone of a mighty organ; and with the final peal of that dreadful anthem there came a sound, as if the roaring wind, the rushing streams, the howling beasts, and every other voice' of the unconverted wilderness were mingling and according with the voice of guilty man in homage to the prince of all. The four blazing pines threw up a loftier flame, and obscurely discovered shapes and visages of horror on the smoke-wreaths above the impious assembly. At the same moment the fire on the rock shot redly forth and formed a glowing arch above its base, where now appeared a figure. With reverence be it spoken, the figure bore no slight similitude, both in garb and manner, to some grave divine of the New England churches.

"Bring forth the converts!" cried a voice that echoed through the field and rolled into the forest.

At the word, Goodman Brown stepped forth from the shadow of the trees and approached the congregation, with whom he felt a loathful brotherhood by the sympathy of all that was wicked in his heart. He could have wellnigh sworn that the shape of his own dead father beckoned him to advance, looking downward from a smoke-wreath, while a woman, with dim features of despair, threw out her hand to warn him back. Was it his mother? But he had no power to retreat one step, nor to resist, even in thought, when the minister and good old Deacon Gookin seized his arms and led him to the blazing rock. Thither came also the slender form of a veiled female, led between Goody Cloyse, that pious teacher of the catechism, and Martha Carrier, who had received the Devil's promise to be queen of hell. A rampant hag was she. And there stood the proselytes beneath the canopy of fire.

"Welcome, my children," said the dark figure, "to the communion of your race. Ye have found thus young your nature and your destiny. My children, look behind you!"

They turned; and flashing forth, as it were, in a sheet of flame, the fiend worshippers were seen; the smile of welcome gleamed darkly on every visage.

"There," resumed the sable form, "are all whom ye have reverenced from youth. Ye deemed them holier than your-selves, and shrank from your own sin, contrasting it with their lives of righteousness and prayerful aspirations heaven-wards. Yet here are they all in my worshipping assembly. This night it shall be granted you to know their secret deeds; how hoary-bearded elders of the church have whispered wanton words to the young maids of their households; how many a woman, eager for widow's weeds, has given her husband a drink at bedtime and let him sleep his last sleep in her bosom; how beardless youths have made haste to inherit their father's wealth; and how fair damsels – blush not, sweet ones – have dug little graves in the garden, and bidden me, the sole guest, to an infant's funeral. By the sympathy of your human hearts for sin ye shall scent out all the places – whether in church, bedchamber, street, field, or forest – where crime has been committed, and shall exult to behold the whole earth one stain of guilt, one mighty blood-spot. Far more than this. It shall be yours to penetrate, in every bosom, the deep mystery of sin, the fountain of all wicked arts, and which inexhaustibly supplies more evil impulses than human power – than my power at its utmost – can make manifest in deeds. And now, my children, look upon each other."

They did so; and, by the blaze of the hell-kindled torches, the wretched man beheld his Faith, and the wife her husband, trembling before that unhallowed altar.

"Lo, there ye stand, my children," said the figure, in a deep and solemn tone, almost sad with its despairing awfulness, as if his once angelic nature could yet mourn for our miserable race. "Depending upon one another's hearts, ye had still hoped that virtue were not all a dream. Now are ye undeceived. Evil is the nature of mankind. Evil must be your only happiness. Welcome again, my children, to the communion of your race."

"Welcome," repeated the fiend worshippers, in one cry of despair and triumph.

And there they stood, the only pair, as it seemed, who were yet hesitating on the verge of wickedness in this dark world. A basin was hollowed, naturally, in the rock. Did it contain water, reddened by the lurid light? or was it blood? or, perchance, a liquid flame? Herein did the shape of evil dip his hand and prepare to lay the mark of baptism upon their foreheads, that they might be partakers of the mystery of sin, more conscious of the secret guilt of others, both in deed and thought, than they could now be of their own. The husband cast one look at his pale wife, and Faith at him. What polluted wretches would the next glance show them to each other, shuddering alike at what they disclosed and what they saw!

"Faith! Faith!" cried the husband, "look up to Heaven, and resist the wicked one."

Whether Faith obeyed, he knew not. Hardly had he spoken, when he found himself amid calm night and solitude, listening to a roar of the wind which died heavily away through the forest. He staggered against the rock, and felt it chill and damp; while a hanging twig, that had been all on fire, besprinkled his cheek with the coldest dew.

The next morning young Goodman Brown came slowly into the street of Salem village, staring around him like a bewildered man. The good old minister was talking a walk along the graveyard to get an appetite for breakfast and meditate his sermon, and bestowed a blessing, as he passed, on Goodman Brown. He shrank from the venerable saint as if to avoid an anathema. Old Deacon Gookin was at domestic worship, and the holy words of his prayer were heard through the open window. "What God doth the wizard pray to?" quoth Goodman Brown. Goody Cloyse, that excellent old Christian, stood in the early sunshine at her own lattice, catechizing a little girl who had brought her a pint of morning's milk. Goodman Brown snatched away the child as from the grasp of the fiend himself. Turning the corner by the meeting-house, he spied the head of Faith, with the pink ribbons, gazing anxiously forth, and bursting into such joy at sight of him that she skipped along the street and almost kissed her husband before the whole village. But Goodman Brown looked sternly and sadly into her face, and passed on without a greeting.

Had Goodman Brown fallen asleep in the forest, and only dreamed a wild dream of a witch-meeting?

Be it so, if you will; but, alas! it was a dream of evil omen for young Goodman Brown. A stern, a sad, a darkly meditative, a distrustful, if not a desperate, man did he become from the night of that fearful dream. On the Sabbath day, when the congregation were singing a holy psalm, he could not listen, because the anthem of sin rushed loudly upon his ear and drowned all the blessed strain. When the minister spoke from the pulpit, with power and fervid eloquence, and with his hand on the open Bible, of the sacred truths of our religion, and of saint-like lives and triumphant deaths, and of future bliss or misery unutterable, then did

Goodman Brown turn pale, dreading lest the roof should thunder down upo. the grey blasphemer and his hearers. Often, awakening suddenly at midnight, he shrank from the bosom of Faith; and at morning or eventide, when the family kelt down to prayer, he scowled, and muttered to himself, and gazed sternly at his wife, and turned away. And when he had lived long, and was borne to his grave, a hoary corpse, followed by Faith, an aged woman, and children and grandchildren, a goodly procession, besides neighbours not a few, they carved no hopeful verse upon his tombstone; for his dying hour was gloom.

P. T. BARNUM

Phineas Taylor Barnum was born in Bethel, Connecticut, USA in 1810. He became a small-business owner in his early twenties, before moving to New York City in 1834. Shortly after arriving, he embarked on an entertainment career with a variety troupe called 'Barnum's Grand Scientific and Musical Theater'. Not long later, Barnum purchased the American Museum, renaming it after himself, and used the museum as a platform to promote a wide range of hoaxes, curiosities and 'freaks, such as the '"Feejee" mermaid' and 'General Tom Thumb', both of which were viewed by over 20 million people.

A brilliant (and shameless promoter), Barnum was constantly accused of fraud, yet quickly became one of the richest men in America. Retiring from show business in 1855, he served as mayor of the town of Bridgeport, where he worked to improve the water supply, bring gaslighting to streets, and enforce liquor and prostitution laws. Later, he was forced through bankruptcy to reopen his American Museum, and in 1971 his famous circus 'The Greatest Show on

Earth' opened in Brooklyn.

Over the course of his colourful life, Barnum authored several books, including *Life of P.T. Barnum* (1854), *The Humbugs of the World* (1865), *Struggles and Triumphs* (1869), and *The Art of Money-Getting*(1880). Although no stranger to using hype or 'humbug' in promotional material as long as the audience was getting value for money, he was contemptuous of those who made money though fraudulent deceptions, and exposed "the tricks of the trade" used by mediums to cheat the bereaved. Barnum died in 1891, aged 80.

H. P. LOVECRAFT

Howard Phillips Lovecraft was born in 1890 in Rhode Island, USA. Although a sickly boy, Lovecraft began writing at a very young age, quickly developing a deep and abiding interest in science. At just sixteen he was writing a monthly astronomy column for his local newspaper. However, in 1908, Lovecraft suffered a nervous breakdown and failed to get into university, sparking a period of five years in which he all but vanished.

In 1913, Lovecraft was invited to join the UAPA (United Amateur Press Association) – a development which re-invigorated his writing. In 1917, he began to focus on fiction, producing such well-known early stories as 'Dagon' and 'A Reminiscence of Dr. Samuel Johnson'. In 1924,

Lovecraft married and moved to New York, but he disliked life there intensely, and struggled to find work. A few years later, penniless and now divorced, he returned to Rhode Island. It was here, during the last decade of his life, that Lovecraft produced the vast majority of his best-known fiction, including 'The Dunwich Horror', 'The Shadow over Innsmouth', 'The Thing on the Doorstep' and arguably his most famous story, 'The Call of Cthulhu'. Having suffered from cancer of the small intestine for more than a year, Lovecraft died in March of 1937.

GORDON MACCREAGH

Gordon MacCreagh was born in Perth, Indiana in 1886. Little is known about his life, other than that he was a keen traveller. He published a number of popular short stories during his lifetime, most of them in the horror genre, including 'Dr. Muncing, Exorcist' (1931), 'The Case of the Sinister Shape' (1932), 'Zimwi Crater' (1934), 'Matto Grosso Fury' (1950) and 'Projection from Epsilon' (1953). Probably MacCreagh's most popular longer work was *White Waters and Black,* an account of his explorations in the Amazon in 1923. An absurd, honest and amusing text, it is regarded by many as one of the great travel books. MacCreagh died in 1953.

NATHANIEL HAWTHORNE

Nathaniel Hawthorne was born in Salem, Massachusetts, USA in 1804. Between 1821 and 1824, he attended Bowdoin College in Brunswick, Maine, along with fellow poet Henry Wadsworth Longfellow and future American President Franklin Pierce. A shy, bookish youth, Hawthorne was writing from a young age, and published his first novel, *Fanshawe,* in 1828. Over the next ten years, he attempted to become a professional writer, supplementing his earnings with a job as a Boston Custom House measurer. In 1842, he married Sophia Peabody and moved to The Manse in Concord, the epicentre of the burgeoning Transcendentalist movement.

Hawthorne's collection of short stories *Mosses from an Old Manse* was published in 1846, and four years later, he published his labour of love, the novel *The Scarlet Letter*. An immediate success, the novel remains widely read to this day, and allowed Hawthorne to devote himself full-time to his writing. Over the rest of his life, he produced six more novels, and a large amount of short stories. Aside from *The Scarlet Letter*, his best-known novel is probably *The Marble Faun*, and his best-remembered short stories include 'My Kinsman', 'Major Molineux', 'Young Goodman Browne' and 'Feathertop'.

Hawthorne died in 1864, following a long period of illness which included bouts of dementia. Though Hawthorne himself was perpetually dissatisfied with his body of work, he remains lauded as one of the greatest American writers, and *The Scarlet Letter* remains a standard school text in the USA. In 1879, Henry James called Hawthorne "the most valuable example of the American genius."

SEABURY QUINN

Seabury Grandin Quinn was born in Washington D.C. in 1889. In 1910, he graduated from law school, and was admitted to the District of Columbia Bar. He served in World War I, and after his Army service became editor of a group of trade papers in New York. His first published work was 'The Law of the Movies' (1917), in *The Motion Picture Magazine*, and his first published fictional story was 'Demons of the Night' (1918), in *Detective Story Magazine*. He introduced the occult detective Jules de Grandin as a character in 1925, and continued writing tales about him until 1951. Quinn's stories were incredibly popular, and between the twenties and fifties he appeared in *Weird Tales* magazine more times than both Robert E. Howard and H. P. Lovecraft. His novel *Roads* was also widely read. Quinn died in old age on Christmas Eve.